ADVANCED

lighthouse 2

Klassenarbeitstrainer

W0390846

Deinen Klassenarbeitstrainer findest du auch in der Cornelsen Lernen App.

Siehst du eines dieser Symbole in deinem Klassenarbeitstrainer, findest du in der App …

- alle **Audios**
- alle **Erklärfilme**
- **Lösungen** zu den Aufgaben

Cornelsen

ADVANCED lighthouse 2

Klassenarbeitstrainer

Im Auftrag des Verlages erarbeitet von
Marc Proulx, Berlin

In Zusammenarbeit mit der Englischredaktion
Klaus Unger (Projektleitung), Chelsea Ledvinka-Heß und Elizabeth Pancake-Steeg, sowie Melina Frick

Beratende Mitwirkung
Katharina Pick, Wülfrath

Lizenzmanagement
Silke Kirchhoff

Illustrationen
Evelt Yanait, Advocate Art
Irina Zinner, Hamburg

Fotos
Anja Poehlmann, Brighton
Für die freundliche Unterstüzung danken wir der *Varndean School, Brighton*

Umschlaggestaltung
Rosendahl, Berlin

Layoutkonzept
Klein & Halm, Berlin

Layout und technische Umsetzung
Compuscript Ireland and Chennai

Audio-Dateien
Studio
Clarity Studio, Berlin
Regie und Aufnahmeleitung
Susanne Kreutzer
Tontechnik
Gislinde Böhringer und Dimitris Kritikos

Druck
Athesiadruck GmbH

PEFC PEFC/18-31-166
PEFC-zertifiziert
Dieses Produkt stammt aus nachhaltig bewirtschafteten Wäldern und kontrollierten Quellen
www.pefc.de

www.cornelsen.de

1. Auflage, 1. Druck 2024
978-3-06-034621-7

Vorwort für Eltern

Sie möchten Ihrem Kind ein sicheres Gefühl für die Klassenarbeiten geben?
Der Klassenarbeitstrainer hilft Ihrem Kind beim Lernen.

Dear Parents,

in den Klassenarbeiten Ihrer Kinder werden die Fertigkeiten Hörverstehen (*Listening*), Leseverstehen (*Reading*), Wortschatz (*Words*), Grammatik (*Language*), Mediation, Lernen lernen (*Study skills*) und Schreiben (*Writing*) abgefragt. Mit dem Klassenarbeitstrainer kann Ihr Kind diese Fertigkeiten gezielt trainieren. Für jede Unit finden Sie verschiedene Aufgaben zu den einzelnen Fertigkeiten.

Im Klassenarbeitstrainer finden Sie darüber hinaus ein Kapitel mit Übungen zur Fertigkeit Sprechen (*Speaking*).

Vorbereitung

Nicht jedes Thema aus dem Schulbuch ist für jeden Lehrplan und für jedes Bundesland relevant, vergewissern Sie sich daher, dass Ihr Kind sich mindestens eine Woche vor der Klassenarbeit genau über die relevanten Themen informiert. Mit einem Lernplan kann Ihr Kind festlegen, wann welche Fertigkeit geübt wird. Eine Vorlage dafür finden Sie auf Seite 6.

More help-Aufgaben

Schreiben stellt für Schülerinnen und Schüler eine besondere Herausforderung dar. Das Kapitel *More help* stellt zusätzliche Hilfen (*useful phrases, switchboxes, etc.*) für die *Writing*-Aufgaben zur Verfügung.

Speaking-Aufgaben

Zwischen den Units 4 und 5 finden Sie Übungen zur Fertigkeit Sprechen (*Speaking*). Manche dieser Übungen kann Ihr Kind allein bearbeiten, andere am besten mit einem Partner (z. B. Klassenkameraden). Damit Sie die Ergebnisse mit den Lösungsvorschlägen vergleichen können, sollte sich Ihr Kind beim Sprechen aufnehmen. Beispielhafte Antworten werden in diesem Klassenarbeitstrainer auch als Audioformat zur Verfügung gestellt.

Lösungen

Wenn eine Aufgabe bearbeitet wurde, kann diese mit den Lösungen aus dem herausnehmbaren Lösungsheft verglichen werden. Achten Sie beim Vergleichen genau darauf, welche Fehler gemacht wurden, und überlegen Sie mit Ihrem Kind, wie diese beim nächsten Mal vermieden werden können. Neben den Beispiellösungen enthält das Lösungsheft auch Lerntipps und die Skripte zu den Hörtexten. Die Bewertungstabelle am Ende jeder Unit hilft Ihnen dabei, den Lernstand Ihres Kindes besser einschätzen zu können.

Achtung

Natürlich enthält jede Unit mehr Aufgaben als eine normale Englischarbeit. Es ist also normal, dass Ihr Kind für die Bearbeitung einer Unit im Klassenarbeitstrainer länger braucht als für eine normale Arbeit.

Wir wünschen viel Spaß beim Lernen und eine erfolgreiche Klassenarbeit.
All the best

So bereitest du dich auf eine Arbeit vor

Damit du dich optimal auf eine Klassenarbeit vorbereiten kannst, musst du lernen, wie du richtig lernst. Das richtige Lernen bzw. Üben wird nicht von der Zahl der bearbeiteten Aufgaben, sondern viel mehr von der Lernatmosphäre und der Strukturierung des Lernprozesses, beeinflusst.

Die Lernatmosphäre vorbereiten

Eine ruhige, druckfreie Lernatmosphäre ist wichtig. Beim Lernen handelt es sich um eine bewertungsfreie Situation, in der das Üben im Vordergrund stehen soll. Es sollte dir möglich sein, angst- bzw. sorgenfrei **Fehler** zu machen und **Fragen** zu stellen. Dies ist wichtig für deinen Lernfortschritt.

Pausen gehören zum Lernprozess, denn sie helfen eine kognitive Überforderung zu verhindern. Auf eine 45-minütige Übungseinheit kann z. B. eine fünf- bis zehnminütige (Bewegungs-)Pause folgen.

Lerninhalte für die Klassenarbeit

Für eine erfolgreiche Vorbereitung ist es wichtig, die **Lerninhalte der Klassenarbeit** zu kennen. Du solltest dich daher mindestens eine Woche vor der Klassenarbeit bei der Fachlehrkraft informieren. Wenn du schon früher mit der Vorbereitung beginnen willst, kannst du im Inhaltsverzeichnis des Schülerbuchs (S. 4–9) nachschauen. Es besitzt eine ausführliche Übersicht über die Kompetenzen und sprachlichen Mittel (*vocabulary* & *grammar*), die du in jeder Unit vermittelt bekommst.

Ergänzende Materialien

Neben dem Klassenarbeitstrainer solltest du ein separates **Lernheft** führen. Dort kannst du die Arbeitsergebnisse zu den Aufgaben festhalten und so jede Aufgabe mehrfach bearbeiten.

Manchmal ist es ebenfalls hilfreich **eine Lernpartnerin oder einen Lernpartner** in der Klasse zu suchen. Ihr könnt euch unterstützen und bei Fragen und Problemen gegenseitig helfen.

Um keine der relevanten Kompetenzen zu vergessen, solltest du einen **Lernplan** erstellen. In diesem kannst du festhalten, was, wann geübt werden soll. Du kannst auch zusätzliche Übungsmöglichkeiten oder hilfreiche Schulbuchseiten notieren. Das Abhaken geübter Kompetenzen gibt dir einen Überblick über den Lernprozess bis zur Klassenarbeit. So könnte ein ausgefüllter Lernplan für Unit 4 aussehen:

Kompetenz / I can...	Sprachliche Mittel	Materialien	Wann übe ich das?	Erledigt?	Noch mal üben?
... talk about celebrations	Voc celebration words	SB, p. 112–113 Vocabulary p. 259	Mo. 20.04.	✓	nein
... describe a special meal	Voc food and drink, a box/carton/jar ... of ...	SB, pp. 114–115 Wordbank, p. 219 Vocabulary, p. 259–261	Mo. 20.04.	✓	ja, am Do. 23.04.
... describe a special meal	G some, any, a little, a few	G SB, p. 116 Language file, p. 206 Erklärfilm in der Cornelsen Lernen App	Di. 21.04.	✓	nein

Um dich gut auf die kommende Englischarbeit vorzubereiten, solltest du dich frühzeitig informieren, welche Themen in der Arbeit drankommen. Damit du nichts vergisst und auch genug Zeit hast, um zu lernen, solltest du dir einen Lernplan erstellen. Du kannst diesen Plan als Vorlage nutzen:

Lernplan von: ______________________________

Datum der Klassenarbeit: ______________________

Unit 1 / 2 / 3 / 4 / 5 / 6

Kompetenz / I can...	Sprachliche Mittel	Materialien	Wann übe ich das? (Datum)	Erledigt? (✓)	Noch mal üben? (ja/nein)

Unit 1
Travel and holidays

1 Listening Sharing holiday stories ______ / 14

▶ SB, pp. 12–13, p. 213

01

a) **Read the task carefully. Then listen to the conversation between Maya and Seth and tick (✓) the right answer – a) or b). One of the questions has two right answers.**
Lies die Aufgabe sorgfältig durch. Höre dann das Gespräch zwischen Maya and Seth an und kreuze die richtige Antwort – a) oder b) – an. Eine der Fragen hat zwei richtige Antworten. (6 Punkte)

Maya ...

1 travelled to ...

☐ a) Italy.

☐ b) Portugal.

2 stayed at ...

☐ a) a campsite.

☐ b) grandma's house.

3 thought it was sometimes too ...

☐ a) sunny.

☐ b) rainy.

Seth ...

4 travelled to ...

☐ a) Scotland.

☐ b) Australia.

5 stayed at ...

☐ a) a campsite.

☐ b) a hostel.

6 thought it was sometimes too ...

☐ a) cloudy.

☐ b) rainy.

b) **Read the sentences below. Listen again. True or false? Tick (✓).**
Lies die untenstehenden Sätze. Höre noch einmal zu. Richtig oder falsch? Hake ab (✓). (8 Punkte)

	true	false
1 Maya was on holiday with her mum and dad.		
2 Summers are always very hot where Maya's grandma lives.		
3 Seth was in Croatia last summer.		
4 There were sunny and rainy days when Seth was at the campsite.		
5 Seth and his family were at the campsite for eight days.		
6 In Edinburgh, Seth's sister was tired.		
7 Maya was in Edinburgh this summer too.		
8 For Seth the festival wasn't very interesting.		

▶ Check

2 READING My Greek holiday ____ / 6

► SB, pp. 15–16

Read Ella's travel blog. *Lies Ellas Reiseblog.*

Lies dir vor dem Lesen des Textes die Aufgabe zum Text gut durch und achte auf Schlüsselwörter. So weißt du, worauf du beim Lesen achten musst.

www.ellas-travelblog.example.net

Friday, July 21

Hi guys! It's day 4 of our holiday in Greece. We're on Kythira now. It's so nice here! We travelled here yesterday from Athens, first by train, then by ferry. But the journey didn't start very well. After breakfast we walked to the train station. It wasn't far from our hotel. But we went the wrong way and got to the station late. We nearly missed our train!

We got off the train at a place called Piraeus. From there we walked to our ferry. It was easy to find because the ferry was so big. Also, a sign in front of it said: "Destination: Kythira".

It was exciting to be on a big ferry. Before we left, they gave a presentation of all the safety equipment on the ferry. That was interesting. After that I took some photos of the sea and the sky. Then we had lunch in the restaurant. In the afternoon we played card games and just relaxed. Later my little brother Benji stood up and said, "This is boring!" He wanted to walk around. When we didn't see him for 20 minutes, Dad and I started to worry. Mum was calm. "I'm sure he's safe," she said. Dad and I went to look for him. We found him in the kid's play area and he wasn't happy to see us. Dad said, "Come on, let's get some ice cream!" Benji agreed. Dad knows how to make us happy. 🙂

We arrived on Kythira late in the afternoon. The ferry took six hours! It's a slow way to travel, but it's cool. I like it. What do you think about ferries? And how do you like to travel?

Bye for now,

Ella

Leave a comment

Complete the sentences. *Vervollständige die Sätze.*

1 Ella and her family travelled to Kythira by ______________________.

2 They got to the station late because they ______________________.

3 When they arrived in Piraeus, they walked ______________________.

4 Before the ferry left, they learned about the ______________________.

5 They were worried about Benji, so they went ______________________.

6 Ella and her family were on the ferry for ______________________.

► Check

3 WORDS Travel experiences ____ / 7

▸ SB, pp. 14–16, pp. 26–27

Complete these comments on Ella's blog with the adjectives in the box. There are three adjectives you don't need. *Vervollständige diese Kommentare auf Ellas Blog mit den Adjektiven im Kasten. Es gibt drei Adjektive, die du nicht brauchst.*

angry • scared • calm • exciting • easy • free • proud • scary • excited • sweet

1 I really enjoyed your blog, Ella! I'm Greek and I'm so ____________ of our amazing ferries.

2 Ferries are cool. They can be big, small, fast or slow. The journey is always ____________ !

3 I was on a ferry in bad weather and it wasn't fun at all, but I learned to be ____________.

4 There's a cute little ferry near my home that you can ride for ____________. I love going on it.

5 We took our dog Waldo on a ferry and he was really scared. Then some people were ____________ at us because he barked so much. It wasn't an ____________ journey.

6 My sister is always ____________ when we ride on ferries. I don't know why. What's so special about them?

4 WORDS A crossword ____ / 10

▸ SB, p. 19, pp. 233–239

Read and look at the clues. Complete the crossword with the right words. *Lies die Hinweise und schaue die Bilder an. Vervollständige das Kreuzworträtsel mit den richtigen Wörtern.*

1 With this ticket you can travel in one direction.

2 Some people do this when they are scared.

3 It's the place at the end of a journey.

4 It's where people stand to get on a train.

5 

6 

7 It's what you wear to a Halloween party.

8 You do this to rest and enjoy your time.

9 

10 When there's no sound, there's only this.

▸ Check

Erklär-film

5 Language Sadie's day ____ / 15

► SB, pp. 14–15, p. 200

Complete Sadie's journal entry with the verbs from the box. Use the correct positive forms of the simple past. There are two extra words. *Vervollständige Sadies Tagebucheintrag mit den Verben aus dem Kasten. Benutze die korrekten positiven Formen des simple past. Es gibt zwei Wörter, die du nicht brauchst.*

arrive • be (2x) • eat • get up • go • have • help • jump • like • listen • play • scream • take • try • watch • win

Saturday, 13th July

What an exciting day! I (1) ______________ early because my team (2) ______________ a game at 9:30 a.m. It (3) ______________ the first game of the summer season and we (4) ______________! We (5) ______________ really well. There (6) ______________ lots of people there to watch us too. After the game Mum and Dad and I (7) ______________ lunch at my favourite burger place. I (8) ______________ a veggie burger for the first time and I really (9) ______________ it! Later I (10) ______________ Dad with the food shopping. We (11) ______________ to my favourite music in the car. That was fun! In the evening after dinner I (12) ______________ the bus to Highgate Cinema to meet Malou and Ethan. They were there when I (13) ______________. We (14) ______________ a scary vampire film and I (15) ______________ so loud!

Erklär-film

6 Language A great summer ____ / 5

► SB, p. 20, p. 201

Alex had a boring summer, but he doesn't want his classmates to know that. Use the negative form and say how his summer really was. *Alex hatte einen langweiligen Sommer, aber er will nicht, dass seine Klassenkameraden das wissen. Benutze die Verneinung und sage, wie sein Sommer wirklich war.*

What Alex says	The real story
1 I went windsurfing every day.	*He didn't* ______________
2 My parents took me to Hollywood and I met Taylor Swift!	______________
3 I learned to fly a plane.	______________
4 I travelled all around England.	______________
5 The zoo gave me a summer job working with the monkeys.	______________

► Check

7 MEDIATION Ghost tour ______ / 6

► SB, p. 16, p. 191

You are on holiday in Northern England and your parents want to visit a castle. Help them understand this information in a travel brochure. Look at the information, then answer your parents' questions.
Du bist im Urlaub in Nordengland und deine Eltern wollen ein Schloss besuchen. Hilf ihnen, diese Informationen in einer Reisebroschüre zu verstehen. Schaue dir die Informationen an und beantworte ihre Fragen.

Experience Chillingham Castle

A long history
Chillingham Castle in Northumberland welcomes you! Enjoy its tall stone towers, wonderful gardens, lakes and parklands. Learn about the long and often horrible history of this great castle on our guided Castle Tour.

Ghost Tour
Chillingham has a history of ghosts too. Many visitors see them walking around the castle halls. On our special Ghost Tour you can experience the castle in the silence and darkness of night – when the ghosts come out.

Opening times
1st April – 5th November
11 am – 5 pm daily
Tickets available from castle ticket office only

Ghost Tour details
For times and dates, see our website.
Ghost Tour ticket price £25.00 for each person
Ghost Tours last 2 hours

Ticket prices*

Adults	£11.00
Children (under 16)	£7.00
Family	£30.00 (2 adults + up to 3 children)

* Prices can change. Please check our website.

1 Was kann man um das Schloss herum sehen?

____

2 Was steht da über die Geschichte des Schlosses?

____

3 „Ghost Tour" verstehe ich schon. Aber was erlebt man dabei?

____

4 Wie sind die Öffnungszeiten für das Schloss? Und wie können wir Karten kaufen?

____

5 Was ist günstiger für uns drei – eine Familienkarte oder drei individuelle Karten?

____

6 Irgendwie reizt mich diese Ghost Tour. Was kostet der Spaß und wann findet die Tour statt?

____

► Check

8 WRITING Gita and Arun in Edinburgh ______ / 15

► More help, p. 81 ► SB, pp. 30–31

Look at the pictures. Then write the story about this sister and brother on their family holiday. Write 100 words or more. Use the simple past. The words in the box can help you. *Schaue die Bilder an. Schreibe dann die Geschichte über den Familienurlaub dieser Geschwister. Schreibe 100 Wörter oder mehr. Benutze das simple past. Die Wörter im Kasten können dir helfen.*

to arrive • to dance • to get off • to see • to shop • to stay • to watch • busy • cheap • cool • excited • exciting • free • fun • clothes • costume • mask • (street) musician • street festival • vampire

____

____

____

____

____

____

____

____

____

____

____

► Check

9 Study Skills **Lost and found** ______ / 7

► SB, p. 30

Linking words can help make a story interesting. Use *or*, *and* or *but* to link the two sentences together.
Verbindungswörter können dazu beitragen, eine Geschichte interessant zu machen. Benutze or, and, *oder* but, *um die beiden Sätze zu verbinden.*

1 It was nearly dark. Their destination was more than a kilometre away.

____

2 She guided the group of kids through the fields. She didn't know the way.

____

3 "Do we turn left at the next road? Do we turn right?"

____

4 Her phone was dead. The little kids in the group didn't have phones.

____

5 "We can stop here and wait for help. We can try to find the way back."

____

6 She hoped for a light or a sound. That's when she heard the noise.

____

7 She wasn't sure what it was. She knew it came from the campsite.

____

Bereich	Aufgabe	erreichte Punktzahl				
listening	1	______ / 14	14–13	12–10	9–7	6–0
reading	2	______ / 6	6	5	4–3	2–0
words	3 4	______ / 7 ______ / 10 } ______ /17	17–16	15–12	11–9	8–0
language	5 6	______ / 15 ______ / 5 } ______ /20	20–18	17–14	13–10	9–0
mediation	7	______ / 6	6	5	4–3	2–0
writing	8	______ / 15	15–14	13–11	10–8	7–0
skills	9	______ / 7	7	6–5	4–3	2–0
Gesamt		______ / 85	85–77	76–60	59–43	42–0

Unit 2
Friends and heroes

1 LISTENING Interesting people ______ / 17

▸ SB, pp. 46–49, p. 214

02

a) **Look at the pictures. How do the four kids look? Listen to the conversation between Ruby and Ellis and match the names with the pictures.** *Schaue die Bilder an. Wie sehen die vier Kinder aus? Höre dem Gespräch zwischen Ruby und Ellis zu und verbinde die Namen mit den Bildern. (4 Punkte)*

b) **Read the sentences. Listen again and complete them.**
Lies die Sätze. Höre noch einmal zu und vervollständige sie. (13 Punkte)

1 Kisi sits ______________________ Ruby in English.

2 She tells really funny ______________________ and always makes Ruby ______________________.

3 Luis doesn't ______________________ to be funny, but Ellis laughs a lot when he's around.

4 He's good at ______________________ and plays on the ______________________ team.

5 Jayden doesn't ______________________ much. He's quiet and a bit ______________________.

6 Ruby likes Jayden because he's ______________________ and helpful when she has ______________________ problems.

7 One day in class Jack was very ______________________ and Vera told him to sit down and be ______________________.

8 Vera wants to become an ______________________.

▸ Check

2 READING A normal hero ____ / 5

► SB, pp. 52–55

Read the text and answer the questions. *Lies den Text und beantworte die Fragen.*

On a cloudy Saturday afternoon, Lyle and Bashir sat in the cinema at Churchill Square. They ate popcorn and watched the teen superheroes Zap and Astrogirl. Zap wore an electric blue costume and a metal mask with a robot eye. Astrogirl had purple hair and wore a black cape and high boots. The pair were funny and confident. They used their amazing superpowers to fight some horrible monsters and, in the end, save New York City.
Outside, after the film, Lyle and Bashir stood with their bikes, ready to ride home.
"Those guys were awesome," Lyle said.
"Yes, they were. It's a shame we don't know any superheroes," Bashir said.
"That's true," Lyle said. He felt very normal, but he dreamed of being a hero.
Just then Lyle saw a man running with a rucksack in his hand. Lyle tried to move out of his way, but the man hit Lyle's bike and fell to the ground. His rucksack flew from his hand.
"Ahh! My leg!" he screamed. He tried to stand up. "Where's my rucksack?!" he said.
Lyle felt bad. "Wait! You're hurt. Let me help you," he said. Lyle took out his phone and called 999. The man looked worried. Lyle tried to keep him calm. Soon the police and an ambulance arrived. People watched and some took photos. The police wrote down Lyle's name and address.

Then they took the man to the hospital.
"I hope I'm not in trouble," Lyle said to Bashir.
The next morning Lyle came into the kitchen. "That was very brave, Lyle," his mum said. "Yes. We read what happened," his dad said.
Lyle was surprised. He saw the newspaper on the table. On the front page it said, "BOY STOPS DANGEROUS THIEF[1]". There was a photo of Lyle with the man on the ground. The article said the man tried to run from police after he took a lot of money in a rucksack. A brave teenager, Lyle B., stopped the man, kept him on the ground, and called the police.
Lyle was shocked. Dangerous? Thief?
"You're a hero, Lyle," his mum said. "We're so proud of you. How do you feel?"
Lyle didn't feel like a hero. "I'm hungry. What's for breakfast?"

[1] **thief** *Dieb*

1 How are Zap and Astrogirl similar?

They are ______________________________

2 Why did the man outside the cinema fall?

____

3 How did Lyle try to help the man?

____

4 What did Lyle's mum say about Lyle? Why did she think this?

____

5 After the film, Lyle "dreamed of being a hero". What happened to his dream after that?

____

► Check

3 WORDS Parts of the body ____ / 10

▶ SB, p. 216

Look at Astrogirl. Write the names of the parts of the body on the numbered lines.
Schaue Astrogirl an. Schreibe die Namen der Körperteile auf die nummerierten Linien.

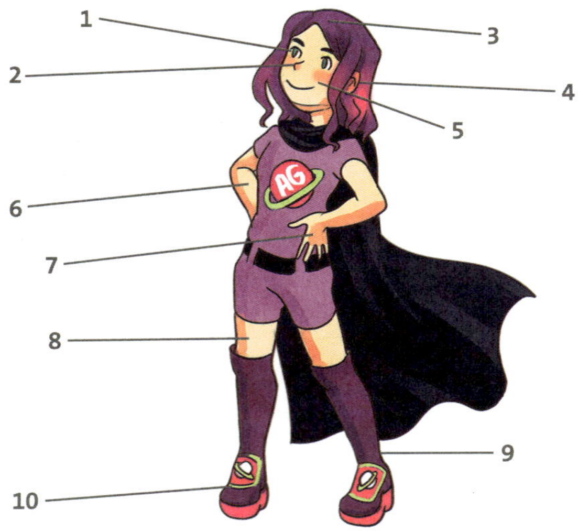

1 ______
2 ______
3 ______
4 ______
5 ______
6 ______
7 ______
8 ______
9 ______
10 ______

4 WORDS That's not right! ____ / 9

▶ SB, p. 54

Read the statements and replace the underlined word with the correct opposite from the box. There is one word too many in the box. *Lies die Aussagen und ersetze das unterstrichene Wort mit dem korrekten Gegenteil aus dem Kasten. Es gibt ein Wort zu viel im Kasten.*

confident • dangerous • hard-working • impatient • rude • tall • tidy • unfair • unhappy • unkind

1 Our parents taught us not to be <u>kind</u> to people. Always help when you can. ______

2 She left without me after I asked her to wait. She's so <u>patient</u>! ______

3 Look at his room – it's not at all messy. I wish my room was this <u>untidy</u>. ______

4 I know she's <u>lazy</u> because she always does her homework on time. ______

5 She said hi to him and he just walked past her. That was so <u>polite</u>! ______

6 Your presentation was great. You looked really <u>shy</u>. ______

7 One reason he's good at basketball is because he's so <u>short</u>. ______

8 Cycling can be <u>safe</u> if you don't wear a helmet. ______

9 He gave her a sweet but he didn't give me one. I thought that was very <u>fair</u>. ______

▶ Check

5 LANGUAGE Meeting a sports hero ____ / 18

► SB, pp. 52–53, p. 202

Katie Dixon, 23, is an Olympic swimmer from Brighton. Her old school invited her for a visit. *Katie Dixon, 23, ist eine olympische Schwimmerin aus Brighton. Ihre alte Schule hat sie zu einem Besuch eingeladen.*

a) **Write the students' questions in the simple past. Then write Katie's short answers.** *Schreibe die Fragen der Schülerinnen und Schüler im simple past. Dann schreibe Katies Kurzantworten. (12 Punkte)*

1 ____________ (you, go) to this school – really? Yes, ____________. Just like you.

2 ____________ (you, wear) a blue uniform too? No, ____________. Mine was red.

3 ____________ (the school, have) a canteen when you were a student? Yes, ____________. I ate there a lot.

4 ____________ (you, walk) to school? No, ____________. I came by bus.

5 ____________ (you, get) lots of homework? Yes, ____________. I didn't like that.

6 ____________ (your parents, make) you swim? No, ____________. I wanted to do it.

!

Fragen im *simple past* bildest du mit *did* und dem Infinitiv des Verbs: *Did you like this school?*
Kurzanworten bildest du mit *did* oder *didn't*: *Yes, I did. / No, I didn't.*
Auch bei Fragen mit Fragewörtern verwendest du bei allen Personen *did* und das Verb im Infinitiv: *When did you go to this school?*

Erklär-film

b) **The students had more questions for Katie. Put the words in the right order.** *Die Schülerinnen und Schüler hatten noch mehr Fragen an Katie. Bringe die Wörter in die richtige Reihenfolge. (6 Punkte)*

1 you / when / learn / did / to swim ? — I learned when I was four.

____

2 become / you / why / a / did / swimmer ? — I love swimming. That's all.

____

3 you / did / how many times / last week / practise ? — Five or six times.

____

4 get ready for / did / you / how / the Olympics ? — I swam a lot, ate well and rested well.

____

5 you / before / did / what / do / each race ? — I listened to quiet music.

____

6 feel / did / to win / how / it ? — It felt amazing!

____

► Check

6 MEDIATION Eine Klassenfahrt ____ / 6

► SB, p. 62, p. 191

Neve, an Irish exchange student in your class, sees this article in the online student newspaper and asks you to help her understand it. Read the article and answer her questions. *Neve, eine irische Austauschschülerin in deiner Klasse, sieht diesen Artikel in der Online-Schülerzeitung und bittet dich, ihr zu helfen, ihn zu verstehen. Lies den Artikel und beantworte ihre Fragen.*

www.schillerschulenews.example.net

Unsere Schule | Unsere Stadt | Sport | AGs | Musik und Film | Leserbriefe | Comics

Eine Klassenfahrt in die Berge *von Linus Kramer*

Letzte Woche hat unsere Klasse – die 9B – einen viertägigen Skiausflug gemacht. Das war aufregend! Die Fahrt mit dem Bus dauerte fünf Stunden. Viele Leute schliefen im Bus ein. Unser Busfahrer war ein cooler Typ mit langen Haaren und Sonnenbrille. Er war auch witzig. Ein paar Mal hat er Witze erzählt und alle zum Lachen gebracht.
Als wir am Hotel ankamen, lag jede Menge Schnee. Es war sonnig und perfekt zum Skifahren!
Am nächsten Morgen bekamen wir unsere Ausrüstung. Die Schüler, die schon gut Ski fahren konnten, brauchten keine Hilfe. Der Rest von uns bekam Skiunterricht. Wir sind viel in den Schnee gefallen und haben viel gelacht, aber wir haben auch viel gelernt.
Leider gab es ein paar Unfälle. Lea ist gestürzt und hat sich den Knöchel verletzt. Und Jonas fuhr einmal zu schnell den Berg hinunter, prallte fast gegen einen Baum und krachte in Yusuf und Sara hinein. Ich habe es gesehen und habe mir große Sorgen gemacht. Yusuf verletzte sich am Bein und konnte für den Rest des Tages nicht mehr Ski fahren. Saras Gesicht war rot und ihre Nase tat weh. Unsere beiden Lehrer, Frau Ramos und Herr Gorek, waren sehr besorgt und hätten beinahe einen Krankenwagen gerufen. Danach haben wir ihnen alle versprochen vorsichtiger zu sein.

1 Neve: I know that "Klassenfahrt" means class trip. How long were they away and where did they go?

You: ____________________

2 Neve: Is he saying that the bus driver was "cool"? Why?

You: ____________________

3 Neve: What was the weather like when they arrived?

You: ____________________

4 Neve: What about the students who didn't know how to ski? What did they do?

You: ____________________

5 Neve: Hey, I know Lea! What does he say about her?

You: ____________________

6 Neve: And what happened to Yusuf and Sara? I see their names 2 times.

You: ____________________

► Check

7 WRITING One of my friends _____ / 15

► More Help, p. 82 ► SB, pp. 46–52, p. 214

Look at the online post about someone's friend. Write a post about one of your friends. *Schaue den Post über eine Freundin von jemandem an. Schreibe einen Beitrag über eine Freundin oder einen Freund von dir.*

Write about:
- what he/she is like (looks, personality)
- how you met
- two reasons why you are happy to be friends with this person

Write 80 words or more.

Schreibe über:
- *was für ein Typ er/sie ist (Aussehen, Persönlichkeit)*
- *wir ihr euch kennengelernt habt*
- *zwei Gründe, warum du froh bist, mit dieser Person befreundet zu sein*

Schreibe 80 Wörter oder mehr.

evie_sundowner43

evie_sundowner43 Ginny and I met at music school last year. She's so creative and she always listens to my ideas. We often write songs ...

► Check

Erklär-film

8 Study Skills Finding the right words ______ / 8

▸ SB, p. 64, p. 185

Read the sentences. Use a word from the same word family as the word in brackets to complete each sentence. *Lies die Sätze. Benutze ein Wort aus der gleichen Wortfamilie wie das Wort in Klammern, um jeden Satz zu vervollständigen.*

Ein Wort gehört immer zu einer Wortfamilie. Kennst du ein Wort aus der Wortfamilie, z.B. das Verb *(to) act*, verstehst du auch die Nomen *action* und *activity* und das Adjektiv *active*. Mit den Regeln zur Wortbildung kannst du die Bedeutung ableiten.

1 We don't eat much fast food because it's ______________________. (health)

2 She wears a helmet because ______________________ is important to her. (safe)

3 I love it in the early morning when our street is ______________________. (silence)

4 Her train is still not here! Did we read the ______________________ time right? (arrive)

5 Thank you for driving us to the station. That is very ______________________. (help)

6 — What does ______________________ mean for you?
— For me it means family and good friends. (happy)

7 When I saw the accident and the woman on the ground, I was ______________________. (shock)

8 At the ______________________ of the film, Zap and Astrogirl are walking home from school. (begin)

Bereich	Aufgabe	erreichte Punktzahl				
listening	1	_____ / 17	17–15	14–12	11–9	8–0
reading	2	_____ / 5	5	4	3	2–0
words	3	_____ / 10 } _____ / 19	19–17	16–13	12–10	9–0
	4	_____ / 9				
language	5	_____ / 18	18–16	15–12	11–9	8–0
mediation	6	_____ / 6	6	5–4	3	2–0
writing	7	_____ / 15	15–14	13–11	10–8	7–0
skills	8	_____ / 8	8–7	6	5–4	3–0
Gesamt		_____ / 88	88–79	78–62	61–44	43–0

▸ Check

Unit 3
Activities and games

1 LISTENING Planning a visit ______ / 12

▶ SB, pp. 78–79

03

a) **Yusuf's cousin Selma is going to visit him in Brighton next weekend. They're making plans on the phone. Listen to their conversation. Number the five activities they choose in the correct order. There are three extra pictures.** *Yusuf's Cousine Selma wird ihn nächstes Wochenende in Brighton besuchen. Sie machen Pläne am Telefon. Höre ihrem Gespräch zu. Nummeriere die fünf Aktivitäten, die sie auswählen, in der richtigen Reihenfolge. Es gibt drei zusätzliche Bilder. (5 Punkte)*

Mache dir kurze Notizen auf einem Notizzettel oder mit Bleistift auf deinem Aufgabenblatt. Bleibe ruhig, wenn du beim ersten Mal nicht alles verstehst. Du hörst den Text meist zweimal.

b) **Read the sentences below. Listen again. True or false? Tick the correct answer (✓).** *Lies die Sätze unten. Höre dann noch einmal zu. Richtig oder falsch? Hake ab (✓). (7 Punkte)*

	true	false
1 Selma's last visit to Brighton was last summer.		
2 Selma is going to arrive in Brighton on Friday at 7 in the evening.		
3 Yusuf's mum is going to make chicken curry for dinner.		
4 The zip wire at Brighton Beach is more expensive than the i360 tower.		
5 Yusuf knows a place where they can eat lunch.		
6 Selma wants to do something in the afternoon that's free.		
7 Selma thinks she's going to be too tired to walk around.		

▶ Check

2 Reading Film reviews ______ / 6

► SB, pp. 84–86, p. 217

It's Saturday evening and Selma and Yusuf want to watch a film online. Read the film reviews. *Es ist Samstag Abend und Selma und Yusuf wollen einen Film online schauen. Lies die Rezensionen.*

Never Stop

Hold on to your seat as three friends go on the adventure of their lives in *Never Stop*. Jenna Colman is in her biggest role as the energetic and sporty Lottie, who finds out that a classmate, Bren, is in trouble. Lottie and her friends Alma and Doro are ready to help. They must find Bren, but time is short and East London is a big, dangerous place. This fast-moving film was an audience favourite at the Redstone Film Festival.
Rating: ★ ★ ★

The Superlatives – Home Sweet Home

The Superlatives, your favourite cartoon superhero family, are back again! Flashman, Supernova, Pixie Pop and Airdot are just trying to do what superheroes do – save the world. It's their job! But life's other challenges, like homework, dating, bad hair and tidying the kitchen, keep getting in the way. *The Superlatives – Home Sweet Home* is the funniest superhero film ever. Try not to laugh out loud.
Rating: ★ ★ ★ ★ ★

Play for your life

In *Play for your life* Kid Walker lives inside a video game where he and his friend Amelia must find their way through dangerous worlds – dark forests, underwater cities full of sea monsters and far-away planets. With each click and each new world, Kid faces new dangers. Amazing special effects, weird characters and a clever story make *Play for your life* one of the best sci-fi films of the year.
Rating: ★ ★ ★ ★

Read the reviews and answer the questions. *Lies die Rezensionen und beantworte die Fragen.*

1 Who is the main character in *Never Stop*?

____

2 Where does *Never Stop* take place?

____

3 What is *The Superlatives – Home Sweet Home* about?

____

4 If you like cartoons, which film should you see?

____

5 Why is *Play for your life* one of the best sci-fi films of the year?

____

6 Which film has a worse rating than *Play for your life*? Which film has the best rating?

____

► Check

3 Words An amazing evening ____ / 9

► SB, pp. 251–259

Beth is writing about a special summer event for her school's online newspaper. Complete the sentences with the correct words from the box. There are two words you don't need. *Beth schreibt über ein besonderes Sommerereignis für die Online-Schülerzeitschrift ihrer Schule. Vervollständige ihre Sätze mit den korrekten Wörtern aus dem Kasten. Zwei der Wörter brauchst du nicht.*

artists • attention • book • challenge • created • energetic • energy • prepared • professional • seat • theatre

Something special is happening at the Brighton Pavilion. If you enjoy a mixture of music, street dance and (1) ____________, then don't miss *Streetbeats*. It's more than a musical. The sounds, colours and costumes are so special. The dancing is great too. It's fast and (2) ____________. Alma Luna and Joe Cooper are the two (3) ____________ who (4) ____________ *Streetbeats*. I saw their first show three years ago, but it wasn't as (5) ____________ as this one. It's clear that Alma, Joe and their group (6) ____________ a lot for this show. *Streetbeats* is only playing for two more weeks, so (7) ____________ your tickets now. My tip: get a (8) ____________ near the front of the theatre, where you can feel the amazing (9) ____________ of this show.

4 Words Music, films and shows ____ / 8

► SB, pp. 86–87, pp. 254–255

Spell the word that matches the description. The letters and lines can help you. *Buchstabiere das Wort, das zu den Beschreibungen passt. Die Buchstaben und die Linien können dir helfen.*

1 This is what you watch to find out what a film is like. t _ _ _ _ _ _
2 These are people who watch a film or show. _ _ d _ _ _ _ _
3 In this kind of film or show, people sing a lot. _ _ _ _ _ _ l
4 Without these, action films can be boring. _ p _ _ _ _ _
(tip: two words) _ f _ _ _ _ _
5 These are the words of a song. _ y _ _ _ _
6 This describes something that is not good at all. _ e _ _ _ _ _ _
7 This is where a story finishes. _ _ _ _ _ g
8 This is a person in a film or a story. c _ _ _ _ _ _ _ _

► Check

5 WORDS **Finding Amelia** ____ / 7

► SB, pp. 88–89, p. 100, p. 255

In the video game version of *Play for your life*, Kid Walker must follow directions to find his friend Amelia. Match the directions and the pictures. *In der Videospiel-Version von* Play for your life, *muss Kid Walker den Wegbeschreibungen folgen, um seine Freundin Amelia zu finden. Ordne die Wegbeschreibungen den richtigen Bildern zu.*

1 Go across the bridge.
2 Turn left at the wall.
3 Go straight on.
4 Go up the stairs.
5 Turn right.
6 Go through the forest.
7 Go past the big tree.
8 Go down the hill.

1	2	3	4
5	**6**	**7**	**8**
A			

Erklär-film

6 LANGUAGE **What do you think?** ____ / 8

► SB, pp. 84–86, p. 205

Compare the three things or activities. Write one comparative and one superlative sentence. *Vergleiche die drei Sachen oder Aktivitäten. Schreibe einen komparativen und einen superlativen Satz.*

1 **loud:** acoustic music – pop music – rock music: *I think that pop music is louder than acoustic music. But rock music is the loudest.*

2 **exciting:** action films – thrillers – sci-fi films: ____________________

3 **funny:** game shows – cartoons – comedies: ____________________

4 **good:** pizza – sushi – fish and chips: ____________________

5 **cool:** footballers – musicians – actors: ____________________

► Check

Erklär-film

7 Language Activity week ____ / 13

► SB, pp. 80–83, pp. 203–204

Longhill High School is having an assembly. The head teacher, Mrs Harrison, is talking to students about next week's Activity Week. *Die Longhill High School hält eine Versammlung. Die Schulleiterin, Frau Harrison, redet mit den Schülern und Schülerinnen über die Activity Week, die nächste Woche ist.*

!

Mit *going to* ... sagst du, was du vorhast oder planst. *I'm going to make a cake.*
Going to hat hier nichts mit dem deutschen „gehen" zu tun, sondern bedeutet „werden."

a) **Complete Mrs Harrison's statements with the correct form of the going to-future.** *Vervollständige die Aussagen von Frau Harrison mit der korrekten Form des going to-future. (8 Punkte)*

1 Next week we ______________________ (have) Activity Week at our school.

2 It ______________________ (not, be) like last year, when we only had activities on some days.

3 You ______________________ (do) different activities every day.

4 Our first day ______________________ (be) fun with lots of games and activities.

5 You ______________________ (not, have) classes in the afternoon.

6 Two popular rappers ______________________ (teach) you how to make rap music.

7 And Mr Shaw, a professional football trainer, ______________________ (explain) why teamwork is important in sports and in life.

8 But I ______________________ (not, tell) you any more now. Wait and see!

b) **Complete the students' questions to Mrs Harrison and her short answers. Use the correct form of the going to-future.** *Vervollständige die Fragen der Schüler und Schülerinnen an Frau Harrison und ihre Kurzantworten. Benutze die korrekte Form des going to-future. (5 Punkte)*

1 Question: ______________________ (we / do) activities all week?
Answer: Yes, ______________________.

2 Q: ______________________ (we / eat) lunch at the normal time?
A: That's a good question. No, ______________________. You're going to eat a bit later.

3 Q: When ______________________ (Mr Shaw / give) his talk?
A: At 2 p.m. on Monday.

4 Q: How ______________________ (we / get) the schedule of activities every day?
A: I'm going to ask your teacher to put the schedule on the board in your classroom.

5 Q: ______________________ (you / open) the canteen for snacks?
A: No, ______________________. But you can bring healthy snacks from home if you'd like.

► Check

8 Mediation A noisy cafe ______ / 10

► SB, pp. 84–85, p. 191

You're visiting London with your parents. You're sharing a table in a busy cafe with a chatty English woman. The cafe is noisy and your parents can't understand everything, so you help them. *Du besuchst London mit deinen Eltern. Ihr Teilt euch einen Tisch in einem hektischen Café mit einer gesprächigen englischen Frau. Das Café ist laut und deine Eltern können nicht alles verstehen, also du hilfst ihnen.*

Woman Are the cafes in Germany as noisy as this one?

Mum Was hat sie gesagt?

You Sie fragt, (1) ______________________________

____

Mum Sag ihr bitte, dass sie noch lauter sind.

Dad Ach nein, sie sind nicht so laut wie hier.

You My mum says (2) ______________________________

______________________________, but my dad says

(3) ______________________________

Woman Oh, how funny! So are you enjoying London?

Mum Sind wir was?

You Sie will wissen, (4) ______________________________

Mum Oh, yes! Erm, ich finde es sehr spannend.

Dad Ach. Ich denke, es ist zu hektisch. Zu viele Autos und Busse und zu viele Menschen.

You (5) ______________________________

(6) ______________________________

Woman I agree with your dad. Are you going to visit any museums?

Dad Das habe ich nicht mitbekommen.

You Sie stimmt dir zu, Papa. (7) ______________________________

Mum Yes, erm, morgen werden wir zum British Museum gehen. Aber heute Nachmittag werden wir noch mit dem Bus zu Covent Garden fahren. Bitte sag ihr das, Schatz.

You (8) ______________________________

____

Woman Covent Garden? You can walk from here – it's not far. Just turn left and go past Wyndham's Theatre, then you turn right and walk straight on. You can't miss it!

You Sie meint, (9) ______________________________

Dad Super! Laufen ist viel besser als mit dem Bus fahren. Bitte bedanke dich bei ihr.

You (10) ______________________________

► Check

9 WRITING It's going to be cool! _____ / 15

► More help, p. 83 ► SB, pp. 80–83

You're texting with a classmate who wasn't at the school assembly today. Look at the timetable and answer her questions about sports week. Name at least three activities that you're going to do. For each activity think about what, when and where. *Du schreibst eine SMS an eine Schulkameradin, die heute nicht bei der Schulversammlung war. Schaue den Zeitplan an und beantworte ihre Fragen zur Sports Week. Nenne mindestens drei Aktivitäten, die du tun wirst. Für jede Aktivität denke an was, wann* und *wo.*

SPORTS WEEK			
	ASSEMBLY HALL	**GYM**	**SPORTS FIELD**
MON	12:45 Sports Week assembly	1:00 Fun with gymnastics 2:30 Gymnastics level 1	1:00 Football level 1 2:30 Golf level 1
TUES	12:45 Table tennis level 1 2:15 Table tennis level 2	12:45 Basketball level 1 2:15 Volleyball level 1	12:45 Cricket level 1 2:15 Tennis level 1
WED	12:45 Judo level 1 2:15 Judo level 2	12:45 Volleyball level 2 2:15 Gymnastics level 2	12:45 Football level 2 2:15 Tennis level 2
THURS	12:45 Boxing level 1 2:15 Boxing level 2	12:45 Basketball level 2 2:15 Gymnastics final	12:45 Cricket level 2 2:15 Cricket final
FRI	12:45 Table tennis final 2:15 Judo final	12:45 Basketball final 2:15 Volleyball final	12:45 Football final 2:15 Tennis final

Did they talk about sports week at the assembly today? What activities are you going to do? Hey, let's do an activity together! Maybe tennis, if it's in the timetable?

► Check

10 Study Skills That's my opinion ______ / 7

▸ SB, p. 96, p. 194

Complete the dialogue with the correct words and parts of phrases from the box. There is one phrase you don't need. *Vervollständige die Dialoge mit den korrekten Wörtern und Satzteilen aus dem Kasten. Es gibt einen Satzteil, den du nicht brauchst.*

> I agree • I don't agree • my opinion • that isn't true •
> You're right • don't think • think • do you think

Amal Why do people worry so much about screen time? In (1) ______________________, there's nothing bad about spending four hours at a computer or tablet.

Sam Hm. For me (2) ______________________. Four hours at a screen is not good for your eyes.

Jess (3) ______________________ with Sam. I get a headache after just one hour on my phone.

Amal But Jess, the screen on your phone is much smaller. That's why you get a headache.

Jess (4) ______________________. It is smaller than a tablet or computer screen. But too much time in front of any screen is just not healthy. What (5) ______________________, Danny?

Danny I (6) ______________________ maybe everybody is different. Maybe four hours of screen time is fine for Amal but not fine for somebody else.

Sam I (7) ______________________ so. That's not what I read online.

Amal OK, guys. I'm going to research this question. Then we can discuss it more.

Bereich	Aufgabe	erreichte Punktzahl					
listening	1	______ / 12		12–11	10–9	8–6	5–0
reading	2	______ / 6		6	5	4–3	2–0
words	3	______ / 9	______ /24	24–22	21–17	16–12	11–0
	4	______ / 8					
	5	______ / 7					
language	6	______ / 8	______ /21	21–19	18–15	14–11	10–0
	7	______ / 13					
mediation	8	______ / 10		10–9	8–7	6–5	4–0
writing	9	______ / 15		15–14	13–11	10–8	7–0
skills	10	______ / 7		7	6–5	4	3–0
Gesamt		______ / 95		95–86	85–67	66–48	47–0

▸ Check

ADVANCED lighthouse 2

Klassenarbeitstrainer

Lösungen

Cornelsen

Unit 1 Travel and holidays

01

1 Listening Sharing holiday stories

Hörtext

Seth How were your summer holidays, Maya?
Maya Oh, really nice.
Seth Where were you?
Maya I was in Portugal with my mum and dad. We visited my grandma.
Seth Oh, that sounds nice. What was the weather like?
Maya It was sunny and really hot every day.
Seth Wow. Are summers always like that in Portugal?
Maya They're sunny and warm, but they're not always that hot. Not in my grandma's town.
Seth Were you at the beach a lot?
Maya Yeah. We were there almost every day.
Seth When we were in Croatia last summer it was really hot too. We ate a lot of watermelon and ice cream!
Maya We were lucky because my grandma's house is nice and cool inside. I was almost never outside in the afternoon. It was too hot. That was boring sometimes. What about you, Seth? Where were you in the summer holidays?
Seth I was in Scotland with my sister and my dad.
Maya Ooh, I like Scotland. Were you in a holiday apartment?
Seth No, first we were at a campsite near Ben Nevis – the big mountain.
Maya Cool! Was it nice?
Seth For the first few days it was really nice. The weather was sunny and we were outside all the time. But then it rained for two days. That wasn't much fun.
Maya How long were you there?
Seth We were at the campsite for eight days. Then we went to the Edinburgh Festival.
Maya Edinburgh! We were there last summer! I loved it. What was it like for you?
Seth We were there for two days. Lots of visitors were in the city for the festival. We stayed in a busy hostel. My sister was tired and ready to go home, but for me it was exciting watching all the street artists.
Maya Wow. What a great holiday!

a)

Maya ...

1 travelled to ...

☐ a) Italy.

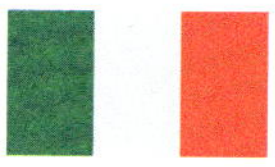

☑ b) Portugal.

2 stayed at ...

☐ a) a campsite.

☑ b) grandma's house.

3 thought it was sometimes too ...

☑ a) sunny.

☐ b) rainy.

Seth ...

4 travelled to ...

☑ a) Scotland.

☐ b) Australia.

5 stayed at ...

☑ a) a campsite.

☑ b) a hostel.

6 thought it was sometimes too ...

☐ a) cloudy.

☑ b) rainy.

b)

	true	false
1 Maya was on holiday with her mum and dad.	✓	
2 Summers are always very hot where Maya's grandma lives.		✓
3 Seth was in Croatia last summer.	✓	
4 There were sunny and rainy days when Seth was at the campsite.	✓	
5 Seth and his family were at the campsite for eight days.	✓	
6 In Edinburgh, Seth's sister was tired.	✓	
7 Maya was in Edinburgh this summer too.		✓
8 For Seth the festival wasn't very interesting.		✓

2 Reading **My Greek holiday**

1 train and ferry • **2** went the wrong way • **3** to the ferry • **4** safety equipment • **5** to look for him • **6** six hours

3 Words **Travel experiences**

1 proud • **2** exciting • **3** calm • **4** free • **5** angry; easy • **6** excited

Nutze unterschiedliche Möglichkeiten, um englische Texte zu hören. Wähle etwas aus, was dir gefällt, z. B. dein Lieblingslied oder dein Lieblingsbuch als Hörbuch auf Englisch. Schaue Filme und Serien auf Englisch. Blende Untertitel ein, falls du Probleme beim Verstehen hast. Blende sie aus, wenn du dich sicherer fühlst oder eine Episode schon mehrfach gesehen hast.

4 WORDS A crossword

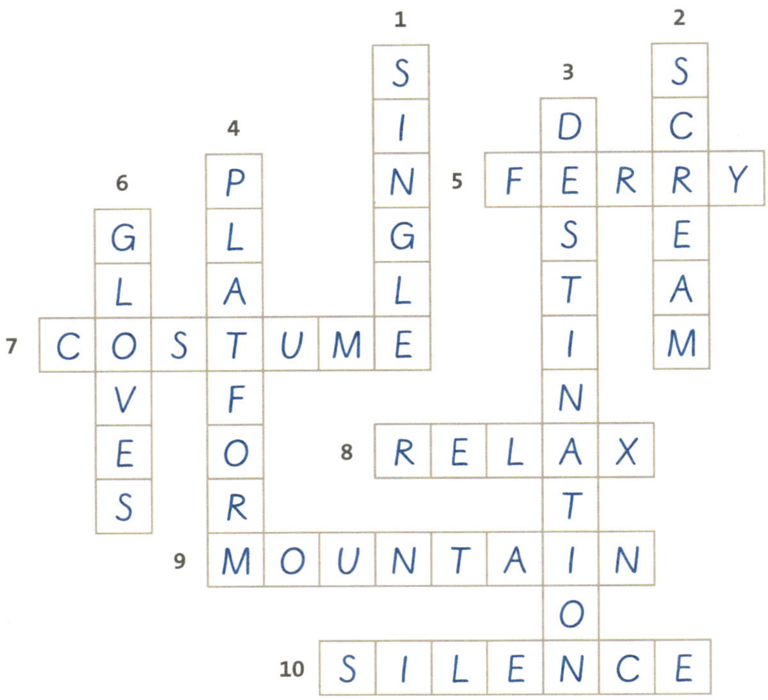

5 LANGUAGE Sadie's day

1 got up • **2** had • **3** was • **4** won • **5** played • **6** were • **7** ate • **8** tried • **9** liked • **10** helped • **11** listened • **12** took • **13** arrived • **14** watched • **15** screamed

6 LANGUAGE A great summer

1 He didn't go windsurfing every day.
2 His parents didn't take to him Hollywood and he didn't meet Taylor Swift.
3 He didn't learn to fly a plane.
4 He didn't travel all around England.
5 The zoo didn't give him a summer job working with the monkeys.

!
Wenn Didi kommt, muss Ede gehen!

7 MEDIATION Ghost tour

1 Es gibt Gärten, Seen und eine große Parkanlage.
2 Es hat eine lange und oft grausame Geschichte. Geister sind auch Teil seiner Geschichte.
3 Man kann das Schloss am Abend besuchen, wenn es still und dunkel ist und die Geister rauskommen.
4 Es hat täglich von 11 bis 17 Uhr auf. Man kann Karten nur vor Ort kaufen.
5 Zusammen gerechnet lohnt sich eine Familienkarte für uns nicht. Individuelle Karten sind insgesamt günstiger.
6 Sie kostet 25 Pfund pro Person. Man muss auf der Webseite schauen, wann die Touren stattfinden.

8 WRITING Gita and Arun in Edinburgh

Benutze die Checkliste um zu kontrollieren, ob du die Aufgabe erfüllt hast.

Does your text ...

describe what happens in all the pictures?	*ja = 2 Punkte pro Bild* *zum Teil = 1 Punkt pro Bild*	
picture 1	train station • to arrive • to get off	____/ 2
picture 2	hostel • cheap • to stay • bed	____/ 2
picture 3	to watch • street artist/musician • see • poster • free	____/ 2
picture 4	clothes • cheap • to shop • costume	____/ 2
picture 5	disco • theatre • costume	____/ 2
picture 6	vampire • cool • exciting • mask • to dance	____/ 2
have about 100 words?	*> 85 Wörter = 3 Punkte* *70–85 Wörter = 2 Punkte* *< 70 Wörter = 1 Punkt*	____/ 3
		Total: ____/ 15

(Lösungsbeispiel)

Their train arrived at the station in Edinburgh and Gita and Arun got off the train with their mum and dad. They walked to a cheap hostel near the station. At McPurdy's Hostel, Arun relaxed in his bed while his dad changed his clothes. Gita and her mum looked at some information about the Edinburgh Festival. Later the family walked around in the city and watched the street artists. Then Gita and Arun saw a poster for a free costume disco. They liked the idea. They went to a second-hand clothes shop and shopped for cheap clothes for costumes. That evening, Gita and Arun went to the costume disco while their parents went to the theatre. At the disco, there was a band and lots of people in costumes danced to their music. The musicians were in costumes too. It was very cool and exciting. Gita and Arun danced all evening and had a lot of fun.

9 STUDY SKILLS Lost and found

1 It was nearly dark and their destination was more than a kilometre away.
2 She guided the group of kids through the fields, but she didn't know the way.
3 "Do we turn left at the next road or do we turn right?"
4 Her phone was dead and the little kids in the group didn't have phones.
5 "We can stop here and wait for help or we can try to find the way back."
6 She hoped for a light or a sound and that's when she heard the noise.
7 She wasn't sure what it was, but she knew it came from the campsite.

Unit 2 Friends and heroes

02

1 LISTENING Interesting people

Hörtext

Ruby I think we're lucky this school year, Ellis. There are so many cool students.
Ellis Yeah, it's great. School is a lot more fun when there are interesting kids around.
Ruby Yeah, like Kisi. She's a lot of fun.
Ellis Wait. I forget. Who is Kisi?
Ruby You know. She's tall and has straight, black hair that she wears in a ponytail.
Ellis Does she sit next to you in English?
Ruby Yes, that's her. She tells really funny jokes and always make me laugh.
Ellis That makes me think of Luis. He doesn't try to be funny, but he knows how to have a good time. I laugh a lot when he's around. You know Luis, right?
Ruby Is Luis in our class?
Ellis No, he isn't. I know him from the basketball team. He's quite tall and wears glasses.
Ruby Oh, him. He's really good at sports. Right?
Ellis Yeah, that's Luis.
Ruby Do you know Jayden? I think he's a friend of Luis's.
Ellis Hm, Jayden. Let me think. What does he look like?
Ruby He's not very tall and he has long, curly hair.
Ellis I think I know him. I tried to talk to him in the canteen one day, but he was very quiet.
Ruby He's a bit shy. We're in the computer club together. I like Jayden because he's always patient and helpful when I have computer problems. He's really good with computers.
Ellis I forgot that you're in the computer club. Do you know Vera? She has short red hair and braces.
Ruby Oh, sure, I know Vera. She sits with us in the canteen sometimes.
Ellis I like her. She's so strong and confident. Did you know she likes climbing?
Ruby Really? I'm not surprised.
Ellis I remember that day in class when Jack was rude to the teacher and Vera told him to sit down and be quiet. I thought that was very brave.
Ruby Yeah, she doesn't like it when people are unfair or mean.
Ellis She told me she wants to be an activist when she grows up.
Ruby That's the perfect job for her!

Die Aufgaben stehen in der Regel in der gleichen Reihenfolge, in der die entsprechenden Stellen im Text vorkommen.

a)

b)

1 next to • **2** jokes; laugh • **3** try • **4** sports; basketball • **5** talk; shy • **6** patient; computer • **7** rude; quiet • **8** activist

2 READING A normal hero

(Lösungsbeispiele)

1 They are funny and confident. They have superpowers too.
2 He ran into Lyle's bike. / He hit Lyle's bike.
3 He called 999 and he tried to keep the man calm.
4 Lyle is "brave" and "a hero" because he stopped a dangerous thief.
5 The newspaper and his mum said he was a hero, but he didn't feel like one.

3 WORDS Parts of the body

1 eye • **2** nose • **3** head/hair • **4** ear • **5** face • **6** arm • **7** hand • **8** leg • **9** ankle • **10** foot

4 WORDS That's not right!

1 unkind • **2** impatient • **3** tidy • **4** hard-working • **5** rude • **6** confident • **7** tall • **8** dangerous • **9** unfair

5 LANGUAGE Meeting a sports hero

a)

1 Did you go ...? Yes, I did.
2 Did you wear ...? No, I didn't.
3 Did the school have ...? Yes, it did.
4 Did you walk ...? No, I didn't.
5 Did you get ...? Yes, I did.
6 Did your parents make ...? No, they didn't.

b)

1 When did you learn to swim?
2 Why did you become a swimmer?
3 How many times did you practise last week?
4 How did you get ready for the Olympics?
5 What did you do before each race?
6 How did it feel to win?

6 Mediation Eine Klassenfahrt

1 Yes, it was a class trip. They went to the mountains for four days.
2 Yes. The bus driver had long hair and sunglasses. He was also funny.
3 There was snow on the ground and it was sunny. It was perfect for skiing.
4 They got lessons. They fell a lot and laughed a lot. But they also learned a lot.
5 Lea fell and hurt her ankle.
6 Jonas went too fast and hit them. Yusuf hurt his leg and Sara hurt her nose.

Du muss nicht 1:1 übersetzen.
- Sage es anders: Wenn du ein Wort nicht kennst, versuche es mit anderen Wörtern zu umschreiben.
- Sage es kurz: Bilde kurze und einfache Sätze, um Fehler zu vermeiden.

7 Writing One of my friends

Benutze die Checkliste um zu kontrollieren, ob du die Aufgabe erfüllt hast. Hast du etwas über die folgenden Themen geschrieben? Gib dir drei Punkte für jedes Thema, das du erwähnt hast .

Did you write about...			✓
what the person looks like?	long/short • straight/curly • blond/dark/red • hair blue/brown/green • eyes braces • glasses		
what the person is like?	brave • clever • confident • creative • fair • friendly • funny • generous • independent • hard-working • kind • patient • practical • relaxed • reliable • shy • sociable		
how you met?	The first time we met was ...• I think we met at/when ... • We became friends when/after/ ...		
two reasons why you are happy to be friends with this person?	He/She	helps me • listens to me • never gets too angry/excited/stressed • teaches me a lot	
	We	have fun together • laugh a lot • like the same things • share everything	
		Total: ______/ 15	

(Lösungsbeispiel)

One of my friends is Herr Werner. He's the trainer for our football club. He's tall and has short, blond hair. He often wears jeans and a T-shirt with the name of our football club on it. He's always very relaxed and really nice. He's also a very clever trainer. I think we met at my first football practice. I like him because he never gets too excited when we play a game and he always makes us feel like winners, even when we don't win.

8 Study Skills Finding the right words

1 unhealthy • **2** safety • **3** silent • **4** arrival • **5** helpful • **6** happiness • **7** shocked • **8** beginning

03

1 LISTENING Planning a visit

Hörtext

Yusuf I'm excited, Selma!
Selma Me too! I can't remember the last time I visited you and your family.
Yusuf I think it was last summer.
Selma I don't think so, Yusuf. Last summer you came here.
Yusuf Oh, you're right! But it was some time last year. How are you going to get here this time?
Selma I'm going to take the train. It arrives at 7 p.m. on Friday.
Yusuf Great. We can come and get you from the train station.
Selma Cool!
Yusuf Let's make some plans, Selma. On Friday evening Dad is going to cook chicken curry for dinner. After that we can just hang out and play video games. Is that OK?
Selma Sure!
Yusuf What about on Saturday? Any ideas?
Selma Yes. I'd like to check out that zip wire at Brighton Beach.
Yusuf The Beach Zip? That's really fun. But it's not cheap.
Selma What's cheaper – the zip wire or the Brighton Viewing Tower?
Yusuf Oh, the Viewing Tower is a lot more expensive.
Selma Then let's go on the zip wire. Mum and Dad are going to pay for it.
Yusuf OK, cool. We can do that in the morning when it isn't so full of people.
Selma And after that, if it's OK, I'd like to walk around Brighton Palace Pier. The last time I was there was such a long time ago.
Yusuf That's perfect, because my favourite fish and chips shop is near the pier. We can get some lunch there after we walk around a bit.
Selma I love fish and chips.
Yusuf This place makes the best in the world.
Selma Great! But in the afternoon we should do something that doesn't cost money.
Yusuf I agree. Hey, I have a great idea!
Selma What is it?
Yusuf I'm going to give you a walking tour. Brighton is full of amazing street art and I can show you where the best street art is.
Selma That sounds like fun! I want to photograph it all for my social media page.
Yusuf We're going to be tired after that, cousin.
Selma Yeah – but the best kind of tired. What are we going to do on Sunday?
Yusuf I have one or two ideas. First, we ...

a)

b)

	true	false
1 Selma's last visit to Brighton was last summer.		✓
2 Selma is going to arrive in Brighton on Friday at 7 in the evening.	✓	
3 Yusuf's mum is going to make chicken curry for dinner.		✓
4 The zip wire at Brighton Beach is more expensive than the i360 tower.		✓
5 Yusuf knows a place where they can eat lunch.	✓	
6 Selma wants to do something in the afternoon that's free.	✓	
7 Selma thinks she's going to be too tired to walk around.		✓

2 Reading **Film reviews**

1 The main character is Lottie.
2 It takes place in East London.
3 A superhero family with the same problems as normal families.
4 If you like cartoons, you should see *The Superlatives – Home Sweet Home*.
5 It has amazing special effects, weird characters and a clever story.
6 *Never Stop* has a worse rating than *Play for your life*. *The Superlatives – Home Sweet Home* has the best rating.

Je mehr englische Texte du liest, desto größer wird dein Wortschatz und desto schneller und besser verstehst du Texte.

3 Words **An amazing evening**

1 theatre • **2** energetic • **3** artists • **4** created • **5** professional • **6** prepared • **7** book • **8** seat • **9** energy

4 Words Music, films and shows

1 t r a i l e r
2 a u d i e n c e
3 m u s i c a l
4 s p e c i a l e f f e c t s
5 l y r i c s
6 t e r r i b l e
7 e n d i n g
8 c h a r a c t e r

Checkliste Vokabeln lernen

- ✓ Lerne nur 5–10 Vokabeln auf einmal.
- ✓ Lerne jeden Tag 10 Minuten.
- ✓ Lerne zusammen mit Freunden. Das macht mehr Spaß.
- ✓ Lerne unterwegs mit einer Vokabellern-App.
- ✓ Schreibe schwierige Wörter auf (mehrmals!).
- ✓ Sprich die Wörter und nimm dich mit dem Handy auf.

5 Words Finding Amelia

1	2	3	4
E	F	C	B
5	**6**	**7**	**8**
A	G	D	H

6 Language What do you think?

(Lösungsbeispiel)

2 I think that thrillers are more exciting than action films. But sci-fi films are the most exciting.
3 I think cartoons are funnier than game shows. But comedies are the funniest.
4 I think sushi is better than pizza. But fish and chips are the best.
5 I think musicians are cooler than footballers. But actors are the coolest.

7 Language Activity week

a)

1 're/are going to have
2 isn't / is not going to be
3 're/are going to do
4 is going to be
5 aren't / are not going to have
6 are going to teach
7 is going to explain
8 'm/am not going to tell

b)

1 Are we going to do …? Yes, you are.
2 Are we going to eat …? No, you aren't.
3 When is Mr Shaw going to give …?
4 How are we going to get …?
5 Are you going to open …? No, I'm/we're not.

8 MEDIATION A noisy cafe

(Lösungsbeispiel)

1 ... ob die Cafés in Deutschland so laut wie dieses Café sind.
2 ... they're even louder, ...
3 ... they're not as loud as here.
4 ... ob ihr London genießt.
5 My Mum thinks it's very exciting.
6 But my dad thinks it's too busy, with too many cars and buses and people.
7 Werden wir noch irgendwelche Museen besuchen?
8 Yes, tomorrow we're going to go to the British Museum. But this afternoon we're going to take the bus to Covent Garden.
9 ... wir können dorthin laufen. Es ist nicht weit.
10 Thank you for your help.

Achte auf kulturelle Unterschiede: Versetze dich in dein Gegenüber hinein und überlege, was für diese Person wichtig ist, um die Situation oder die Inhalte verstehen zu können.

9 WRITING It's going to be cool!

Benutze die Checkliste um zu kontrollieren, ob du die Aufgabe erfüllt hast.

Did you ...		
tell your friend that they talked about sports week?	Yes, we did/they did. • we/they talked about ...	_______/ 3
write about what, when and where for at least three activites?	at the sports field • in the assembly hall • in the Gym • at 12:45 • on Monday	*3 Punkte pro Aktivität = 9 Punkte gesamt* _______/ 9
answer your friend's question about choosing tennis together?	We can ... • I like your idea. • How about we ... • Let's do ...	_______/ 3
		Total: _______/ 15

(Lösungsbeispiel)

Yes, they talked about Sports Week next week. It's going to be cool! On Monday I'm going to play golf at 2:30 at the sports field. I can't wait! On Tuesday I'm going to play table tennis level 1 at 12:45 in the assembly hall. Would you like to do football level 2 at 12:45 on Wednesday at the sports field? And I like your idea too! Tennis is in the timetable. We can play tennis level 1 on Tuesday at 2:15. Does that sound good?

10 STUDY SKILLS That's my opinion

1 my opinion • **2** that isn't true • **3** I agree • **4** You're right • **5** do you think • **6** think • **7** don't think

04

1 LISTENING Celebrating with friends

Hörtext

Myra Hi Danny!

Danny Hey, Myra. You're right on time.

Myra I'm so excited!

Danny You really are. Have you ever been to the festival before?

Myra No, I haven't. This is my first time.

Danny You're going to love it. The others are going to meet us in the park at one o'clock, before the music starts.

Myra Right. When does the fun start with all the colours?

Danny That comes later.

Myra Oh, OK. Alex and Ellie have both texted me. Alex is going to bring a few bottles of lemonade and Ellie says she can bring some paper cups.

Danny That's perfect. It's going to be hot today.

Myra And I talked to Jenna this morning. She wants to bring some biscuits.

Danny Sounds good. I saw Tariq yesterday. He's going to come, but he's not sure what he's going to bring.

Myra So, Danny, do you have the ... you know?

Danny Of course! That's the most important thing! It's in my rucksack.

Myra Cool! Here comes the bus. Let's go!

Danny This looks like a good place. I brought a picnic blanket to sit on.

Myra Good idea. Well, we're on time. Where is everybody?

Danny Somebody is texting me. ... It's Tariq. He's going to be a bit late.

Alex Hey guys!

Myra Alex! Hi!

Alex Good to see you. Where are the others?

Danny They haven't arrived yet.

Alex Ah, this is great. I'm going to take off my shoes, it's so warm. Look what I've brought. Nice and cold.

Myra Ah, the lemonade! Thanks, Alex!

Ellie Hey everybody!

Danny Hi Ellie! You're wearing white clothes. That's great!

Ellie Yes. And because everything is white, I stay cooler.

Alex It's not going to be white for very long – not after the fun begins.

Ellie I know. I can't wait!

Myra Have you brought the paper cups?

Ellie Oh no! I've left them at home!

Alex Don't worry, Ellie. I've brought some. I think we have enough.

Myra Yay! Well done, Alex! Oh, my phone ... oh no, Jenna can't come. Her mum is sick and needs her help.

Danny That's a shame. That means no biscuits.

Myra Well, did you think I wouldn't bring anything?

Ellie What's that in the plastic box, Myra?

Myra Ta-da!

Danny Ahh, biscuits!

Alex Hey, look over there. Do you see that? The musicians are getting ready.

Ellie I can't wait to dance. And look, here comes Tariq!

Tariq Hi, sorry I'm late.

Alex	Hey, Tariq. It's OK. We've just got here too.
Myra	What's in the bag, Tariq?
Tariq	Some chocolate cake. My mum baked it this morning.
Alex	Great! The party can begin.
Myra	Well, nearly. Show them what you have in your rucksack, Danny.
Danny	Yep. Look at these.
Ellie	What are they?
Danny	They're packets of coloured powder! I've brought enough for everybody!
Myra	Look at those colours! Now we can celebrate!
All	Yeah! Woo-hoo!

a)

1 Notting Hill Carnival

2 Holi

3 Guy Fawkes Night

4 Eid al-Fitr

b)

1 the park; one o'clock • **2** bus • **3** be (a bit) late • **4** take off his shoes • **5** white clothes • **6** mum is sick (and needs her)

c)

1 H • **2** B; G • **3** C; F • **4** E • **5** D • **6** A

2 Reading **Hello from Brighton**

1 Amir is two years younger that Frida.
2 It (only) takes a few minutes.
3 She felt nervous because she didn't know anybody.
4 He welcomed her and made some jokes.
5 School is hard because she doesn't understand everything that the teachers say.
6 They celebrated Eid al-Fitr.
7 They brought something delicious to eat.

3 WORDS Guy Fawkes Night

1 sunset • **2** suddenly • **3** somebody • **4** strange • **5** took off • **6** scared • **7** time to go • **8** put on • **9** fireworks • **10** each other • **11** embarrassing

4 WORDS My favourite food

2 a carton of milk • **3** a piece of cheese • **4** a tin of baked beans • **5** a pot of yoghurt • **6** a box of chocolates • **7** a bottle of orange juice • **8** a packet of biscuits

5 LANGUAGE Work before play

a)

2 Senna and Ryan have already finished their homework.
3 Senna has already found the Guy Fawkes masks.
4 Ryan has already fed the dog.

b)

6 Ryan hasn't done the shopping yet.
7 Ryan and Senna haven't made their beds yet.
8 Senna hasn't taken out the rubbish yet.

!

Mit *already* sagst du was **schon** passiert ist. Du verwendest *already* in bejahten Aussagen.

Mit *yet* sagst du was **noch nicht** passiert ist. Du verwendest *yet* in verneinten Aussagen.
Du kannst auch mit *yet* fragen, ob etwas **schon** geschehen ist.

– Have you fed the dog yet?

– Yes. I've already fed the dog his dinner. Look. He hasn't finished eating yet.

6 LANGUAGE Anything you want

1 some • **2** any • **3** some • **4** some • **5** any • **6** some • **7** any • **8** some

7 LANGUAGE Yes, Mum

2 I have • **3** Has the dog been out? • **4** she hasn't • **5** Have they come yet? • **6** they have • **7** Have you bought them yet? • **8** I haven't • **9** I haven't forgotten

8 LANGUAGE Party time

1 a few • **2** a little • **3** a little • **4** a little • **5** a few • **6** a little • **7** a few

9 MEDIATION A special day

1 Sie feiern Saint Patrick's Day. Die Leute tragen grün, und es gibt Paraden.
2 Robyn sagt, dass sie es wirklich einfach feiern, irisch zu sein.
3 Es gibt eine Parade, Straßenkünstler, Märkte und irische Musik überall.
4 Sie war mit Freunden unterwegs. Sie haben ihre Gesichter grün angemalt und haben lustige Kostüme angezogen. Sie schickt uns Fotos.

10 Writing A birthday celebration

Benutze die Checkliste um zu kontrollieren, ob du die Aufgabe erfüllt hast. Gib dir drei Punkte für jede Frage, die du mit „ja“ beantwortest. Wenn du die Aufgabe nur zum Teil erfüllt hast, gib dir zwei Punkte.

Did you ...		✓
write about all four things listed under "today"?	• arrive at Auntie Nicky's house • surprise Granny with birthday cake • have big family dinner • play board games	
use simple past to write about the things that happened "today"?	We **arrived** ... at 11 a.m. At 2 p.m. we **surprised** ... Then we **had** a big dinner. Later we **played** board games.	
write about all four things listed under "tomorrow"?	• go hiking with Granny Ann • Dad makes fish and chips for lunch • visit art museum with cousins • Dad and I drive back to Brighton	
use going to-future to write about the plans for "tomorrow"?	I**'m going to go** hiking ... in the morning. Dad**'s going to make** ... for lunch. My cousins and I **are going to visit** ... At 4 p.m. we**'re going to drive** ...	
use a least 3 words or phrases from the word box?	birthday cake • beef/lamb/pork • to arrive early/on time • to blow out the candles • to give sb. a present • to have sth. for dinner • to make a wish • to surprise sb. • to thank sb.	
		Total: ______/ 15

(Lösungsbeispiel)

Hey Allie, it's going great. We arrived on time at 11 a.m. We had a fun day. In the afternoon we surprised Granny Ann with a birthday cake. She made a wish and blew out the candles – well, most of them. After that we gave her presents and she thanked everybody. At 5:30 we had a big family dinner. We had lamb and it was delicious! Later we played board games and laughed a lot.

Tomorrow morning (at 10 a.m.) I'm going to go hiking with Granny Ann. I must remember to take a water bottle. I always get thirsty! Then (at 12) Dad is going to make fish and chips for lunch. After that my cousins and I are going to visit an art museum. At 4 p.m. Dad and I are going to drive back to Brighton.

11 Study Skills A Chinese celebration

(Lösungsbeispiel)

CHINESE NEW YEAR

- *clean and decorate at home*
- *special foods*
- *fireworks and parades*

05

1 MONOLOGUE A celebration (Unit 1, Unit 4)

(Lösungsbeispiel)

I remember I celebrated the end of the last school year with the kids in my class. We had a big picnic. Our teacher was there and a lot of parents were there too. I went there with my dad. The celebration was in a city park. Everybody brought some kind of food or drink. I brought some cheese sandwiches and a big bowl of strawberries. The picnic was a lot of fun. We played football and we sang karaoke. For me the karaoke was the best. I didn't like the football so much because it was too hot on that day.

06

2 MONOLOGUE Giving directions (Unit 3)

(Lösungsbeispiel)

Turn right on Castle Road, then turn left on Victoria Street. Go past the museum and take the next left on Barley Road. Then take the second leftand you'll see the street market on your left.

Alle Lösungsbeispiele aus diesem Kapitel kannst du in der Cornelsen Lernen App abspielen.

07

3 MONOLOGUE An interesting person (Unit 2, Unit 5)

(Lösungsbeispiel)

My Aunt Lisa is a really interesting person. She has brown hair that's long and curly, and her eyes are brown too. She's short, like my dad. Aunt Lisa is clever and creative and very funny. She's a cook in a restaurant, so she's good at preparing food, but she's also good at organizing things and thinking fast. I like Aunt Lisa because she's very sociable and she's always friendly and kind to me and to other people.

08

4 DIALOGUE A good teacher (Unit 2)

(Lösungsbeispiel)

Partner A What do you think? What makes a good teacher?
Partner B I think a good teacher has to be very patient and well-organized.
Partner A Well, I think it's important that a teacher is friendly.
Partner B I don't agree. He or she should be kind, but it's not important to be friendly.
Partner A Why do you think that a teacher doesn't have to be friendly?
Partner B Because students often don't work hard when the teacher is too friendly.
Partner A OK. A teacher doesn't have to be friendly, but he or she should be kind and fair.
Partner B Yes, I agree. And I like teachers who are well-organized. What do you think?
Partner A Yes, that's important.
Partner B Great. Then we agree on three things that are important for a good teacher: he or she should be well-organized, kind and fair.
Partner A Yes.

09

5 DIALOGUE Making plans (Unit 3)

(Lösungsbeispiel)

Partner A Let's do something together this weekend!
Partner B OK, great! What are we going to do?
Partner A On Saturday we could go to the street market and shop for second-hand clothes.
Partner B That's a good idea, but I'd like to go to the trampoline park too. They have a special price this weekend. It's only £3. We could go after the street market. It stays open until 6 p.m.
Partner A OK, that's fine. So first we're going to go to the street market in the morning. Then we can go to the trampoline park in the afternoon. What about after that?
Partner B What about the skatepark? There's a skate competition at 3 p.m. We could go there a bit later.

Partner A I don't really want to go there after trampolining. We're going to be tired. Let's do something quieter. What about the comic book club? That's in the evening. It's a lot of fun. And this week it's all about superheroes, my favourite.
Partner B I like that idea! Superheroes are so cool.
Partner A Great. Hey, on Sunday afternoon some school friends are going to have a beach clean-up party. I'd like to go. What about you?
Partner B That sounds good! Let's do it!

10 6 DIALOGUE In a clothes shop (Unit 5)

(Lösungsbeispiel)

Partner A Hello, can I help you?
Partner B Yes, please. I'm looking for some trainers.
Partner A We have these blue trainers here.
Partner B Those are nice. I'd like to try them on.
Partner A What size are you?
Partner B I need size 40.
Partner A Right. Here's a size 40. You can try them on here.
Partner B Thank you. I like these!
Partner A I think they're your size.
Partner B I'll take them. How much are they?
Partner A They're 45 pounds. Would you like to pay by card or cash?
Partner B I'll pay by card.
Partner A OK. ... Here's your receipt.
Partner B Thank you.
Partner A You're welcome. Goodbye!

Let's talk (Schulbuch, S. 223-227) enthält Wendungen für wichtige Situationen, wie z. B.: Sich verabreden und etwas planen.

11

1 LISTENING I want to be a ...

Hörtext

Dad How was school today, Luis?
Luis It was OK. We had a guest speaker in our class – an architect. He talked to us about his job and what he does.
Mum That sounds interesting. Do you think you'd like to be an architect?
Luis Hm. I don't think so. But I know that Anna wants to be one. She had lots of questions for him.
Dad Why does Anna want to be an architect?
Luis She told me that she wants to design really cool houses.
Dad It's a challenging job, but Anna is creative and she's practical too. I think she'll be successful.
Mum What do your other friends want to be?
Luis Nick wants to be a cook and have his own restaurant.
Mum That's great! I'm not surprised. Nick is so ambitious.
Luis He's just discovering cooking. He helps his parents in the kitchen a lot and he loves it.
Dad You should be more like Nick, Luis, and help in the kitchen.
Luis Ha-ha. I've heard that the restaurant business is very busy and hard.
Dad Yes, you have to be energetic and hard-working.
Luis Oh, and Melanie wants to be a footballer. That's not surprising. It's all she talks about.
Mum If she's good, she'll make a lot of money as a professional.
Dad But she has to be confident and strong. It's a hard sport, and women footballers still don't earn as much as the men.
Alma I want to be a footballer and play for England!
Mum Oh, Alma, I'm sure you'll be a great footballer.
Luis But Alma, you told me you wanted to be an artist and paint big pictures.
Alma I did? Oh yeah, I did. You're right – I want to be an artist!
All (laughter)
Dad What about you, Luis? Have you thought about what you want to be?
Luis Yes, sure.
Mum When you were little you wanted to be a police officer.
Luis That was a long time ago, Mum. Now I want to be a nurse.
Mum Interesting. Why a nurse?
Luis It looks like an exciting job. And every day you're helping and saving people.
Dad Being a nurse is an important job. You have to be calm and reliable because you're working with people who need your help.
Luis Do you think I'll earn enough money?
Mum Maybe not as much as an architect or a professional footballer, but I'm sure you'll be fine.

a)

Anna: C architect
Nick: E cook
Melanie: A footballer
Alma: G artist
Luis: D nurse

b)

1 creative; practical • **2** ambitious; restaurant • **3** energetic; hard-working • **4** confident; strong • **5** calm; reliable

2 Reading What do you do with your pocket money?

(Lösungsbeispiel)

1 He puts a few pounds in a jar every week.
2 She buys treats for her rabbits and she goes to the cinema.
3 His hobby is building things that fly.
4 It's expensive.
5 She spends it on cool activities and events.

3 Words Chores

4 Words Jobs in the family

a)

1 H vet • **2** C firefighter • **3** F programmer • **4** G shop assistant • **5** D hairdresser • **6** A banker • **7** I writer

b)

(Lösungsbeispiel)

1 Cousin Kate designs the coolest houses.
2 Aunt Frida gets up very early to bake the best bread and cakes.

5 Words My favourite aunt

1 look forward to • **2** curious • **3** doesn't mind • **4** solve • **5** came true • **6** earns • **7** comfortable • **8** successful • **9** generous

6 Language Seeing into the future

1 'll/will work • **2** 'll/will share • **3** won't/will not go • **4** will walk • **5** will be • **6** won't/will not earn • **7** won't/will not know • **8** will spend • **9** 'll/will remember • **10** won't/will not have • **11** will help • **12** will come • **13** 'll/will get • **14** will move

7 LANGUAGE I love chores

1 forgets • **2** won't have • **3** know • **4** won't forget • **5** 'll/will miss • **6** start • **7** explain • **8** 'll/will understand • **9** swap • **10** 'll/will do • **11** 'll/will be • **12** need

Nicht jedes Thema aus deinem Schulbuch ist für alle Schulformen relevant. Informiere dich daher rechtzeitig vor der Klassenarbeit bei deiner Fachlehrkraft über die relevanten Inhalte.

8 LANGUAGE At the market

1 Luca and I went to the street market on Saturday. / On Saturday Luca and I went to the street market.
2 Luca often buys second-hand clothes.
3 I usually get some delicious street food.
4 I spent nearly five pounds at a fish and chip stand this time. / This time I spent nearly five pounds at a fish and chip stand.
5 Luca bought two T-shirts at the big clothes stand after lunch. / After lunch Luca bought two T-shirts at the big clothes stand.

9 MEDIATION In a shop

1 Do you have rain jackets?
2 ... sie haben sie in verschiedenen Farben: grün, blau, schwarz und rot.
3 She would like a green one.
4 Grün is sehr beliebt. Sie haben nur noch einige in Größe S.
5 S ist too small for her. Do you have a blue one in size M?
6 Das ist eine blaue in M.
7 She likes the blue jacket (more than the green one). How much is it?
8 Sie kostet £43,95.
9 She'll take it.
10 Möchten Sie bar oder mit Karte bezahlen?
11 She would like to pay by card.

10 WRITING A big change

Benutze die Checkliste um zu kontrollieren, ob du die Aufgabe erfüllt hast.

Did you ...			
use all the notes from the list?	- Mum > better job - Me > a new adventure - miss Brighton - be hard to leave you all	- my new school > be good - kids and teachers > be nice - not live near the sea - have a house with a garden	*1 Punkt pro Notiz = 8 Punkte* _____/ 8
use the will-future at least 4 times?	I'll/It'll/They'll/We'll ... • I/it/we/they won't ...		_____/ 4
use at least 3 words or phrases from the box?	I think/hope ... • I'm sure ... • It's a shame that ... • Let's ... • move • stay in contact • look forward to ... • sad • strange • different • interesting • ...		_____/ 3
			Total: _____/ 15

(Lösungsbeispiel)

Hi guys,

I have some sad news. My mum has a new job in Leeds, so we're going to move there in the summer. Mum will have a better job, so that's good. For me it will be a new adventure. I'm sure some things will be different and other things will be the same. But I'll miss Brighton! It will be hard to leave you all. I hope that my new school will be good and that the kids and teachers there will be nice. Leeds will be very different, I'm sure. It's a shame that we won't live near the sea. But maybe we'll have a house with a garden. Let's stay in contact, guys! I look forward to texting and having video calls often with you.

Bye for now,

Manu

11 Study Skills **Check your writing**

a)

1 Does the email start and end correctly? yes ☐ no ☑

2 Is the email friendly and personal? yes ☑ no ☐

b)

<u>Rosie</u>
How are you? I hope that <u>you enjoying</u> the summer break. It feels strange to be here in Leeds. Our new house is great and I've already met a few nice <u>neahbours</u>, but I miss <u>brighton</u>. Here I don't know anybody, so it's boring. And I don't feel comfortable riding my bike here because <u>I the city don't know</u>.
I'm looking <u>forword</u> to starting school. Then I'll make some friends and I won't feel so alone. I've already <u>saw</u> my new school. It's not very big, so I hope it'll be easy to meet people.
I miss you, Rosie! Let's have a video chat soon.
<u>Manu</u>

Hi/Hey/Dear Rosie,

you are enjoying

neighbours; Brighton

I don't know the city.

forward

seen

Bye (for now)/See you,

💡

Ein Text ist noch nicht fertig, wenn du ihn zu Ende geschrieben hast. Du solltest ihn noch mehrmals durchlesen bzw. in Partnerkorrektur durchlesen lassen.

Im *Skills file* (Schulbuch, S. 183) findest du wichtige Informationen zum Überprüfen und Verbessern von Texten.

Unit 6 The treasure hunt

12

1 LISTENING A good boy

Hörtext

Laura Freddie! Freddie, where are you? Freddie? Where is he?
Miles Hi, Laura. Are you looking for Freddie?
Laura Hi, Miles. Yes, I wanted to take him for a walk. Or have you already gone out with him today?
Miles No, I haven't. I saw him this morning in the garden before I went to school. That was the last time.
Laura Where could he be?
Miles I was in the corner shop on my way home and had a chat with Mr O'Neill. He said he saw Freddie through the shop window about an hour ago, with one of the kids from the neighbourhood. You know how Freddie likes to play with the younger kids.
Mum Hello? Anybody home?
Miles We're in here, Mum.
Mum Ah, hello, you two.
Laura Hi, Mum. We're just talking about Freddie. He's outside somewhere, but we don't know where.
Mum Oh, that dog. Let's not worry about it. He'll come home soon. He always does.
Miles Yeah, that's what I think.
Mum I just saw Mrs Wong who lives down the road. She asked if I've seen her son, Tommy. He's late for his music lesson and she's worried because he's never late. Have you seen him around the neighbourhood?
Miles Tommy Wong? He's the boy that Mr O'Neill saw with Freddie! The two of them have gone somewhere together.
Laura Do you hear that? It sounds like Freddie!
Miles It's him! He's back.
Mum There. I told you!
Laura Freddie! There you are. Where have you been?
Mum He looks so excited.
Laura It's OK, boy. Quiet down. Why are you so excited?
Miles He can't stop jumping around. It's like he wants to tell us something.
Laura Is it Tommy? Freddie, where's Tommy?
Mum Now he's really excited.
Laura Show us where Tommy is, Freddie! Miles, let's follow him on our bikes.
Miles Yeah! Maybe something has happened!
Laura OK, wait for us, Freddie! We're coming! I've got my phone, Mum. We'll ring you.
Mum OK!
Miles Freddie is running into the forest!
Laura There, look! At the bottom of that hill!
Miles It's Tommy! It looks like he's hurt!
Laura Tommy! Are you OK?
Tommy Man, I'm glad to see you guys. I fell and hurt my ankle. I can't walk.
Miles Don't worry. We'll get help for you.
Laura I'm going to call our mum and she'll call your mum. Everything will be fine.
Tommy Did Freddie show you guys where to find me?
Miles He sure did.
Tommy He's a smart dog. Good dog, Freddie! Thanks a lot.
Laura Yep. You're a hero, Freddie! Good boy! ... OK, you can stop barking now!

a)

b)

		Correction
1	Miles has already taken Freddie for a walk today.	*hasn't taken*
2	Mr O'Neill saw Freddie this morning with a younger kid.	*an hour ago*
3	Mrs Wong told Laura's mum that she's looking for Mr O'Neill.	*(her son) Tommy*
4	When Freddie comes back, he barks and he's hungry.	*excited*
5	Laura and Miles decide to catch Freddie on their bikes.	*follow*
6	Freddie takes them to a field where they find Tommy.	*forest*

2 Reading A girl named Laura

(Lösungsbeispiel)

1 She told him that she was friends with his friend Emily.
2 They met at the library because Laura needed help with maths.
3 Jake saw Emily. He learned that she didn't know Laura.
4 He thought that Laura stole his rucksack. / Laura didn't steal his rucksack.
5 Because Jake found out she that she wasn't Emily's friend. / Because Jake found out that what she said the day before wasn't true.

3 Words Matching

1 H • **2** D • **3** J • **4** I • **5** B • **6** A • **7** F • **8** C

4 Words Nature Walk

1 hike • **2** nature reserve • **3** Good luck • **4** shouted • **5** grass • **6** dandelions • **7** pretty • **8** looked up • **9** pointed at • **10** bench • **11** Congratulations

5 Writing A fun class trip

Benutze die Checkliste um zu kontrollieren, ob du die Aufgabe erfüllt hast. Hast du etwas über die folgenden Themen geschrieben? Gib dir drei Punkte für jedes Thema, das du erwähnt hast.

Did you ...		✓
have a friendly opening and closing?	Dear ... • Hello ... • Hi ... Best wishes, • Bye for now,	
describe a (class) trip that you have been on?	I once did a cool day trip to/with ... My favourite class trip was to ... I went there with ... We were there for ... First we ..., then we ... We were there for ...	
say what you liked about the trip?	It was really fun/cool/interesting because ... The best part was (when we) ... What I liked most was (when we) ... I'll never forget when ...	
tell Dylan if you've ever done a treasure hunt?	I've done a few treasure hunts. I did a treasure hunt at a ... I've never been on a treasure hunt.	
describe something you remember about the treasure hunt? or, if you have never done a treasure hunt, say whether you would like to do one?	I remember that there was/were ... The clues were easy/hard/funny. At the end the treasure was ... I'd like to ... A treasure hunt sounds fun/boring. I think ... sounds better than a treasure hunt.	
		Total: _____/ 15

(Lösungsbeispiel)

Dear Dylan,

Thanks for your email. My favourite class trip was a day trip to Sanssouci Park in Potsdam. That's near Berlin. It's a really big park that's over 150 years old. We had a tour of Sanssouci Palace and we had a picnic in the park. We didn't do a treasure hunt there, but I did a treasure hunt a few years ago at a birthday party. It was a lot of fun, but the clues were too easy. I would really like to do another one!

Bye for now,

Jamal

Unit 4
Celebrate!

1 LISTENING **Celebrating with friends** ______ / 14

► SB, pp. 112–113

04

Read the tasks carefully. Then listen to some friends who meet for a celebration. *Lies die Aufgaben sorgfältig durch. Höre dann den Freunden zu, die sich für eine Feier treffen.*

a) **What are they celebrating? Tick the right picture.** *Was feiern sie? Markiere das richtige Bild. (1 Punkt)*

1 Notting Hill Carnival

2 Holi

3 Guy Fawkes Night

4 Eid al-Fitr

b) **Listen again. Complete the sentences.** *Höre noch einmal zu. Vervollständige die Sätze. (7 Punkte)*

1 The friends agree to meet in ______________________ at ______________________.

2 Danny and Mira arrive there by ______________________.

3 Tariq sends a text message to say he's going to ______________________.

4 When Alex arrives, he decides to ______________________.

5 Ellie is the only one who is wearing ______________________.

6 Jenna can't come because her ______________________.

c) **What do they bring to the celebration? Listen again. Match the people (1-6) with the things (A-H) that they bring – if they bring anything. Some bring more than one thing.** *Wer bringt was zur Feier? Verbinde die Freunde (1-6) mit den Sachen (A-H) die sie mitbringen – wenn sie überhaupt etwas mitbringen. Manche bringen mehr als eine Sache mit. (6 Punkte)*

1 Myra
2 Danny
3 Alex
4 Ellie
5 Jenna
6 Tariq

A chocolate cake
B a picnic blanket
C paper cups
D nothing – she can't come
E nothing – she forgets
F lemonade
G packets of coloured powder
H biscuits

► Check

2 Reading Hello from Brighton ____ / 7

► SB, pp. 122–123, p. 208

Frida is a German exchange student who is living in Brighton for three months. She has written to her English class in Germany. Read her email. *Frida ist eine deutsche Austauschschülerin, die für drei Monate in Brighton wohnt. Sie hat eine Mail an ihre Englischklasse in Deutschland geschrieben. Lies ihre Mail.*

to birgit.bauer@example.edu

from frida.wilhelm@example.net

Hi everybody,

I arrived here two weeks ago and so much has happened already! The Khans, my host family, are really nice. Their daughter Aisha is my age and her brother, Amir, is two years younger than me.

I really like Brighton. It only takes a few minutes by bike from the Khans' house to the beach. That's so cool! They've already shown me a lot of the area. I told Aisha that I feel like I've been everywhere. She said, "You haven't seen anything yet!"

At school it was a bit weird on the first day. I felt nervous because I didn't know anybody. But my class teacher, Mr Whittaker, helped me to relax. He welcomed me and made some jokes. He said, "You speak English better than I do!" We laughed about that. Everyone in my class was really friendly too. But school hasn't been easy. I don't always understand everything that the teachers say and some days it feels like I haven't learned anything.

Last weekend was the end of Ramadan, so the family celebrated Eid al-Fitr. Aisha's cousins and aunts and uncles were there – and everyone brought something delicious to eat. There was music and dancing too. It was an amazing celebration! Check out this photo!

Bye for now, Frida

Answer the questions. Write complete sentences. *Beantworte die Fragen. Schreibe ganze Sätze.*

1 How old is Aisha's brother Amir compared to Frida?

____

2 How long does it take to ride from the Khans' house to the beach?

____

3 Why did Frida feel nervous on her first day of school?

____

4 What did Mr Whittaker do to help Frida on her first day?

____

5 Why is school hard for Frida?

____

6 What did the Khan family do at the end of Ramadan?

____

7 What did the guests bring to the celebration?

____

► Check

3 WORDS Guy Fawkes Night ______ / 11

► SB, pp. 259–266

Tariq is describing an experience that he had. Complete his statement with the words from the box. There are two more words than you need. *Tariq schildert ein Erlebnis. Vervollständige seine Ausssagen mit den korrekten Wörtern aus dem Kasten. Es gibt zwei Wörter, die du nicht brauchst.*

each other • embarrassing • fireworks • knock • put on • scared • somebody • strange • suddenly • sunrise • sunset • took off • time to go

It was Guy Fawkes Night and I was at home, waiting for my friend Alex. We wanted to go to a bonfire. It was nearly dark – just after (1) ______________ – and (2) ______________ there was a sound at our front door. I opened the door and (3) ______________ with a Guy Fawkes mask on stood there in silence. "Hello?" I said. It was a really (4) ______________ moment. Then the person laughed and (5) ______________ the mask. It was Alex! I laughed too. I didn't tell him that he (6) ______________ me. "Come on," he said. "It's (7) ______________." At the bonfire, Alex (8) ______________ his mask again. We stood and watched the fire. Then I heard (9) ______________ above us. "Look!" I said, turning to Guy Fawkes. The mask was silent again. "Oh, stop being weird!" I said. "Are you talking to me?" a girl asked from behind the mask. We looked at (10) ______________. I heard Alex laughing further away. It was so (11) ______________.

4 WORDS My favourite food ______ / 7

► SB, p. 115, p. 219, p. 260

Ms Friedman has asked her class to say what their favourite food or drink is. Complete their statements with words from the two boxes. *Frau Friedman hat ihre Klasse gefragt, was ihr Lieblingsessen oder -getränk ist. Vervollständige die Aussagen der Klasse mit den Wörtern aus den beiden Kästen.*

bottle • box • carton • ~~jar~~ • packet • piece • pot • tin	baked beans • biscuits • cheese • chocolates • ~~honey~~ • milk • orange juice • yoghurt

1 *a jar of honey*

2 ______________

3 ______________

4 ______________

5 ______________

6 ______________

7 ______________

8 ______________

► Check

5 LANGUAGE Work before play ____ / 6

Erklärfilm

► SB, pp. 119–120, p. 141, p. 207, pp. 312–313

Senna (S) and her brother Ryan (R) are excited about Guy Fawkes Night. But there's a lot to do around the house before the celebration. Look at their mum's list of jobs. *Senna (S) und ihr Bruder Ryan (R) freuen sich auf Guy Fawkes Night. Es gibt zuhause aber noch viel zu tun, bevor sie feiern. Schaue dir die Liste von ihrer Mutter an.*

To do before you go	
– clean bathroom (R) ✓	– do the shopping (R)
– put away your clean clothes (S)	– make your beds (R+S)
– finish your homework (S+R) ✓	– take out the rubbish (S)
– find the Guy Fawkes masks (S) ✓	– feed the dog (R) ✓

a) **Say what they have already done (✓). Write three sentences.** *Sage, was sie schon erledigt haben (✓). Schreibe drei Sätze.*

1 Ryan has already cleaned the bathroom.

2 ______

3 ______

4 ______

b) **Now say what they haven't done yet. Write three sentences.** *Sage, was sie noch nicht erledigt haben. Schreibe drei Sätze.*

5 Senna hasn't put away her clean clothes yet.

6 ______

7 ______

8 ______

6 LANGUAGE Anything you want ____ / 8

Erklärfilm

► SB, p. 116, p. 206

Mayil and her dad are getting something to eat and drink at the Holi celebration. Complete their dialogue with *some* and *any*. *Mayil und ihr Papa holen sich etwas zum Essen und Trinken beim Holi-Fest. Vervollständige ihren Dialog mit* some *und* any.

Mayil Can I have (1) ______ cola please, Dad?

Dad No, sorry Mayil, you can't have (2) ______ cola, but you can have (3) ______ tea or juice.

Mayil Can I have (4) ______ cake?

Dad There isn't (5) ______ cake. Would you like (6) ______ biscuits?

Mayil I don't want (7) ______ biscuits, thanks. I'll just have (8) ______ tea.

!

Some (einige, etwas) verwendest du:
– in bejahten Aussagen
– in Fragen, wenn du um etwas bittest oder wenn du jemandem etwas anbietest.

Any (kein, keine, keinen) verwendest du in verneinten Sätzen.

► Check

7 Language Yes, Mum ____ / 8

► SB, pp. 119–121, p. 208, pp. 312–313

Noah is alone at home. His mum is at work. Complete their text messages with the correct form of the present perfect. *Noah ist allein zuhause. Seine Mutter ist bei der Arbeit. Vervollständige ihre Textnachrichten mit der korrekten Form des present perfect.*

Hi Noah. I hope you had a good day at school.
(1) Have you eaten a snack yet? (you / eat / a snack / yet?) ✓

Hi Mum. Yes, (2) ____________. Thanks. ✓

Good. (3) ____________ (dog / be / out?)
She needs to go out to the garden. ✓

No, (4) ____________. I'm going to go out with her now. ✓

Thanks. The party helpers are going to come today.
(5) ____________ (they / come / yet?) ✓

Yes, (6) ____________. They've already put up the decorations. ✓

Oh great. And please don't forget the party snacks.
(7) ____________ (you / buy / them / yet?) ✓

No, I (8) ____________. But don't worry. I (9) ____________ (not forget). ✓

Erklär-film

8 Language Party time ____ / 7

► SB, p. 116, p. 206

Complete the sentences with *a little* or *a few*. *Vervollständige die Sätze mit* a little *oder* a few.

!
zählbare Nomen → a few
unzählbare Nomen → a little

Noah Mum, (1) ____________ guests have just arrived!

Mum Oh dear. I need (2) ____________ more time.

Noah Would you like (3) ____________ help?

Mum Yes, thank you, Noah. Is there (4) ____________ honey in that jar next to you?

Noah No, there isn't. But there are (5) ____________ packets of sugar here.

Mum That's fine. I can mix the sugar with (6) ____________ water. It should only take (7) ____________ minutes. Then we're ready!

► Check

9 MEDIATION A special day ______ / 4

► SB, pp. 112–113, p. 191

The Irish exchange student who stayed with you last year has sent your family a postcard from Cork. Your parents have some questions about it. Read her postcard and answer your parents' questions.

Die irische Austauschschülerin, die letztes Jahr bei dir gewohnt hat, hat deiner Familie eine Postkarte aus Cork geschickt. Deine Eltern haben Fragen dazu. Lies ihre Postkarte und beantworte die Fragen deiner Eltern.

POSTCARD

Hi everybody,
Happy Saint Patrick's Day!
I wanted to share with you the amazing time I've had here today. March 17th is a special day. Of course, it's a celebration of Saint Patrick, but we really just celebrate being Irish! Here in Cork it's the biggest day of the year. Lots of people come here for the parade, but there are also street artists and outdoor markets and there's Irish music everywhere. I've been out with my friends all day. We wanted to have a little fun, so we painted our faces green and put on funny costumes.
I can send you photos!
Bye, Robyn

For Correspondence

Familie Kramer
Kleeblattstr. 14
48143 Münster
Germany

For Address Only

1 Mutter: Das ist lieb von Robyn. Was ist das Besondere am 17. März?

Du: Sie feiern ______________________________.

2 Vater: Aber es geht nicht nur um diesen Sankt Patrick, oder?

Du: Robyn sagt, ______________________________

______________________________.

3 Vater: Also bei ihr in Cork ist es ein großes Event. Das habe ich kapiert. Was passiert denn?

Du: ______________________________

______________________________.

4 Mutter: Ich möchte hören, was Robyn an dem Tag gemacht hat. Was hat sie geschrieben?

Du: ______________________________

______________________________.

► Check

10 WRITING A birthday celebration ______ / 15

► More help, p. 84 ► SB, pp. 114–117, pp. 122–123

Ben and his dad have travelled to Bristol to celebrate his grandma's 70th birthday. Ben's friend Allie texts him late that evening. Read Ben's diary notes and answer Allie's questions. You can use the ideas in the box or your own. *Ben ist mit seinem Vater nach Bristol gereist, um den 70. Geburtstag seiner Großmutter zu feiern. Bens Freundin Allie schreibt ihm spät am Abend eine SMS. Lies Bens Tagebuchnotizen und beantworte Allies Fragen. Du kannst die Ideen im Kasten oder deine eigenen verwenden.*

Granny Ann's birthday

today	tomorrow
11 a.m. – arrive at Auntie Nicky's house	10 a.m. – go hiking with Granny Ann
2 p.m. – surprise Granny with birthday cake	12 a.m. – Dad makes fish and chips for lunch
5:30 p.m. – have big family dinner	1:30 p.m. – visit art museum with cousins
7:30 p.m. – play board games	4 p.m. – Dad and I drive back to Brighton

birthday cake • beef/lamb/pork • to arrive early/on time • to blow out the candles • to give sb. a present • to have sth. for dinner • to make a wish • to surprise sb. • to thank sb.

Hey Ben, how's it going in Bristol? When did you guys arrive? Did your Grandma have a nice birthday? Tell me about it! ✓

____
____
____
____
____
____
____
____
____ ✓

Sounds cool! What's your plan for tomorrow? What time are you going to drive back? ✓

____
____
____
____
____
____
____
____
____ ✓

► Check

11 STUDY SKILLS A Chinese celebration ____ / 4

► SB, pp. 130–131

Emily is giving a presentation about a tradition that her family celebrates. Read her statement and use the information to make a slide. Make the notes on the slide short and clear. *Emily hält eine Präsentation über eine chinesische Tradition, die ihre Familie feiert. Lies ihre Aussage und benutze die Informationen, um eine Folie zu erstellen. Mache die Notizen kurz und klar.*

Chinese New Year celebrates the start of the new year in the traditional Chinese calendar. It takes place on different dates in January and February. People clean their houses and decorate them with red for good luck. Families enjoy special foods during this time and each food has a meaning: happiness, a long life or other good things. There are lots of fireworks and parades with loud drums to scare away monsters and bad luck. The highlight of the parade is often a dragon.

____

- ____________________
- ____________________
- ____________________

Bereich	Aufgabe	erreichte Punktzahl		🤩	😎	🤔	😭
listening	1	____ / 14		14–13	12–10	9–7	6–0
reading	2	____ / 7		7	6–5	4	3–0
words	3	____ / 11	____ /18	18–16	15–12	11–9	8–0
	4	____ / 7					
language	5	____ / 6	____ /29	29–26	25–20	19–15	14–0
	6	____ / 8					
	7	____ / 8					
	8	____ / 7					
mediation	9	____ / 4		4	3	2	1–0
writing	10	____ / 15		15–14	13–11	10–8	7–0
skills	11	____ / 4		4	3	2	1–0
Gesamt		____ / 91		91–82	81–64	63–46	45–0

► Check

Speaking

1 Monologue A celebration (Unit 1, Unit 4)

05

► SB, pp. 14–17, pp. 112–117

Think of the last time you celebrated something. Maybe it was a birthday (yours or someone else's) or a holiday (e.g. Christmas). What can you remember about it? *Überlege, wann du zuletzt etwas gefeiert hast. Vielleicht war es ein Geburtstag (von dir oder einer anderen Person) oder ein Feiertag (z.B. Weihnachten). Woran kannst du dich erinnern?*

Make notes about ...
- what and where you celebrated
- who you celebrated with
- what you brought with you or prepared
- what the celebration was like
- what kind of activities there were
- what you enjoyed
- what you didn't like

You can use these pictures for ideas:

Talk about the celebration. You can start like this:
I remember I celebrated ...
I went to ... at ...
I was with ...
The celebration was in/at ...
I brought/prepared a/some ...

Höre dir die Lösungsbeispiele an und achte nicht nur auf den Inhalt, sondern auch auf Aussprache und Intonation.

► Check

2 MONOLOGUE Giving directions (Unit 3)

06

► SB, pp. 88–90, p. 255

You are on holiday with your family. You're staying in a hostel in Castle Road. At breakfast another guest who doesn't have his phone with him asks you for directions to the street market in Blackwell Road. Look at the map. Draw the way from the hostel to the street market. Then give the man directions from the hostel to the street market.

Du bist mit deiner Familie im Urlaub. Ihr wohnt in einem Hostel in der Castle Road. Beim Frühstück fragt dich ein anderer Gast, der sein Handy nicht dabeihat, nach dem Weg zum Straßenmarkt in der Blackwell Road. Schaue die Karte an. Zeichne den Weg vom Hostel zum Straßenmarkt. Beschreibe dann dem Mann den Weg vom Hostel zum Straßenmarkt.

Nimm dich beim Üben auf. Danach kannst du kontrollieren, ob du wirklich alles gesagt hast, was du sagen wolltest.

You can use the phrases in the box and your own ideas:

Turn left/right at (the) ...
Go across/down/past/through/up (the) ...
Go straight on at (the) ...
When you come to / see (the) ..., then ...
... the first/second/... street on your left/right

► Check

🔊 07

3 MONOLOGUE An interesting person (Unit 2, Unit 5)

► SB, pp. 46–49, p. 146, p. 214

Talk about a person who you like. It can be somebody you know personally, somebody famous, or maybe a fictional character (e.g. from a book, film or TV series). The words and phrases in the box will help you. Circle the words you want to use. *Sprich über eine Person, die du magst. Es kann eine Person sein, die du persönlich kennst, jemand berühmtes oder vielleicht ein fiktionaler Charakter (z.B. aus einem Buch, Film, oder einer TV Serie). Die Wörter und Sätze in der Box werden dir helfen. Umkreise die Wörter, die du nutzen möchtest.*

a) **Think about what he or she looks like. Think about the person's**
– hair
– eyes
– size

black • blond • brown • curly • long • red • short • straight
blue • blue-green • brown • dark • eyes • glasses
short • tall

b) **Think about his or her personality.**

brave • clever • confident • creative • fair • friendly • funny • generous • independent • hard-working • kind • patient • practical • reliable • shy • sociable

c) **Think about what the person does and what he or she is good at.**

actor • artist • builder • bus driver • cook • dancer • footballer • gamer • hairdresser • mechanic • nurse • programmer • student • teacher • writer	
He/She is good at... maths • sports • listening • drawing • organizing things • solving problems	He/She is good with ... children • animals • computers

d) **Talk about this person and what you like about them. Use the words you circled in a), b) and c).**

My Aunt Lisa is a really interesting person. She has brown hair that's long and curly, and her eyes are brown too. She's short, like my dad. Aunt Lisa is ...

► Check

4 Dialogue A good teacher (Unit 2)

08

► SB, pp. 46–51, p. 194, p. 226

It's the end of the school year and you and your partner are talking about the teachers who you thought were good. Look at the list below. What makes a good teacher? Tick three things that you think are important. *Es ist das Ende des Schuljahres und du und dein Partner oder deine Partnerin sprecht über die Lehrkräfte, die ihr gut fandet. Schaut euch die Liste unten an. Was macht eine gute Lehrkraft aus? Hake drei Dinge ab, die du wichtig findest.*

- ☐ clever
- ☐ confident
- ☐ fair
- ☐ friendly
- ☐ funny
- ☐ good at listening
- ☐ good with technology
- ☐ hard-working
- ☐ kind
- ☐ patient
- ☐ smart
- ☐ well-organized

Talk with your partner. Agree on three things that are important for a good teacher.
You can use the ideas in this box or your own:
Sprich mit deinem Partner oder deiner Partnerin. Einigt euch auf drei Dinge, die für eine gute Lehrkraft wichtig sind. Ihr könnt die Ideen aus der Box oder eure eigenen Ideen verwenden:

I think a good teacher should be … • … must be/have … • … has to be/have … •
I like teachers who/that are … • I think / For me it's important that a teacher is … •
That's true, but I think it's more important to be … • I don't think a teacher should be … •
I agree. • I don't agree.

You can start like this:

Partner A *What do you think? What makes …?*

Partner B *I think …*

Partner A *Well, I think it's important that …*

Partner B *I don't agree. He or she must be …*

Partner A *Why do you think that …?*

Partner B *Because …*

Partner A *A teacher doesn't have to …*

Wenn du Dialoge übst, finde ein Gegenüber, mit dem du zusammen üben kannst, am besten jemand aus deinem Englischkurs. Du kannst auch eine Freundin, einen Freund, oder jemanden aus deiner Familie, der Englisch spricht, bitten, mit dir Dialoge zu üben.

► Check

5 DIALOGUE **Making plans (Unit 3)**

09

► SB, pp. 82–83, p. 194, p. 224

You and your partner want to do something together this weekend. Look at the ideas that you have noted down in your phone. *Du und dein Partner oder deine Partnerin wollen dieses Wochenende etwas gemeinsam unternehmen. Schau dir die Ideen an, die du in deinem Handy notiert hast.*

A

- Street market: second-hand clothing
  Saturday, 9 a.m. – 4 p.m.
- Skatepark: skate competition
  Saturday, 3 p.m.
- Beach clean-up party with school friends
  Sunday, 3 p.m.

B

- Trampoline park: special price £3 all weekend
  Saturday and Sunday, 9 a.m. – 6 p.m.
- Comic book club: This week's topic is *Why we love superheroes*
  Saturday evening
- Bike tour by the beach, Sunday at 2 p.m.

Talk with your partner, share your ideas and find out about his or hers. Agree on three things that you'd like to do together. The phrases in the box will help you. *Sprich mit deinem Partner oder deiner Partnerin, teile deine Ideen und finde heraus welche Ideen er oder sie hat. Einigt euch auf drei Dinge, die ihr gerne gemeinsam machen würdet. Die Satzteile in der Box helfen dir.*

I'd like to ... • I (don't) really want to ... • I have a good/better idea! • I think we should ... • Let's ... • That's a good idea. • That's too ... • We could ... • What about a ...? • What about you?

You can start like this:

Partner A *Let's do something together this weekend!*

Partner B *OK, great! What are we going to do?*

Partner A *On Saturday we could ...*

Partner B *That's a good idea, but I'd like to ...*

Partner A *OK, that's fine. So first we're going to ... . What about after that?*

► Check

6 Dialogue In a clothes shop (Unit 5)

10

▶ SB, pp. 155–157, p. 227

Work with a partner and agree on your roles – Partner A or Partner B. Then look at your role cards.
Arbeite mit einem Partner oder einer Partnerin. Einigt euch auf eure Rollen – Partner A oder Partner B. Schaut euch dann eure Rollenkarten an.

Partner A

You are a shop assistant in a clothes shop. Partner B is a customer in your shop. Help the customer choose and pay for one of the items above. You can use the phrases below or your own.

You start.

- *Hello, can I help you?*
- *What size …?*
- *The changing rooms are …*
- *I (don't) think it's your size.*
- *You look …*
- *It is … / They are …*
- *Would you like to try on / look at …?*
- *Would you like to pay by …?*
- *You're welcome.*

Partner B

You are a customer in a clothes shop. Partner A is the shop assistant. You are shopping for one of the items in the illustrations above. You can use the phrases below or your own.

Partner A starts.

- *Yes, please.*
- *I'm looking for … / Do you have …?*
- *I need size …*
- *I'd like to try it on. Where are the …?*
- *I (don't) like …*
- *How much is/are …?*
- *That's fine. / Oh, that's too …*
- *I think I'll …*
- *I'll pay by …*
- *Thank you and …*

When you are finished, swap roles.

▶ Check

Unit 5
Getting ready for the future

1 LISTENING I want to be a ... ______ / 15

► SB, pp. 144–146, p. 221

11

a) **Luis is talking during dinner with his parents and his younger sister Alma about future jobs. Listen to their conversation. Look at the pictures and write the correct letter (A–G) and the job next to each name. There are two extra jobs.** *Luis spricht beim Abendessen mit seinen Eltern und seiner jüngeren Schwester Alma über zukünftige Berufe. Höre ihrem Gespräch zu. Schaue die Bilder an und schreibe den korrekten Buchstaben (A-G) und den Beruf neben jeden Namen. Es gibt zwei zusätzliche Berufe. (5 Punkte)*

A

B

C

D

E

F

G

Anna: ____________________ Nick: ____________________ Melanie: ____________________

Alma: ____________________ Luis: ____________________

b) **Read the sentences carefully. Then listen again and complete the sentences with the correct words in the box. You don't need all the words.** *Lies die Sätze sorgfältig durch. Höre dann noch einmal zu und vervollständige die Sätze mit den korrekten Wörtern aus dem Kasten. Du brauchst nicht alle Wörter. (10 Punkte)*

ambitious • calm • confident • crazy • creative • energetic • happy • hard-working • little • practical • reliable • restaurant • shop • strong

1 Anna will be successful because she's both ____________________ and ____________________.

2 Nick is very ____________________ – he wants to have his own ____________________.

3 In the restaurant business you have to be ____________________ and ____________________.

4 Melanie can do well, but she has to be ____________________ and ____________________.

5 Luis will help people in his job if he is ____________________ and ____________________.

► Check

2 READING What do you do with your pocket money? ____ / 5

▸ SB, pp. 154–155

Read the answers to this question that some students in Brighton have given. Then complete the exercise. *Lies die Antworten auf diese Frage, die einige Schülerinnen und Schüler aus Brighton gegeben haben. Vervollständige dann die Übung.*

Manu

Sometimes I buy sweets or snacks or I buy something for a friend. I also like to shop for used comic books and video games online. But I save some of my money too. Every week I put a few pounds in a big jar in my room. I like watching the jar get fuller and fuller. Maybe in the future I'll buy something bigger with the money. But I can wait. I've read that you have to be patient when you're trying to save.

Jenny

"Save a little, spend a little" – that's what my mum says. I get pocket money every week. Before I can go out and buy something with it, I put half of it in my savings account. Then I can't spend it on anything unimportant. I'm trying to be organized. I like to buy treats for my two rabbits and once a month I go to the cinema with friends. At the moment I'm saving for a new mobile.

Dylan

I spend most of my pocket money on my hobby. My friends think it's weird, but I like building things that fly – especially small planes and drones. I'm really curious about how they work and it's cool to try to create my own. But it's an expensive hobby – there's always something more I need to buy. Luckily my uncle helps me. He has the same hobby and I can buy things from him second-hand.

Eve

Sometimes I buy clothes with my pocket money, but only when there's something that I really want. It's nice to have things, but I want to spend my money on cool activities and events like concerts, sports games, rides and museums. It's just more fun. So I try to stay away from shopping centres. Everything there says "Buy me! Buy me!" It's hard. You have to be strong.

Answer the questions. *Beantworte die Fragen.*

1 How does Manu save some of his pocket money every week?

____

2 What does Jenny spend her pocket money on when she's not saving?

____

3 What is Dylan's hobby?

____

4 What is one problem Dylan has with his hobby?

____

5 What does Eve like to spend her money on the most?

____

▸ Check

3 Words Chores ______ / 8

► SB, pp. 150–151, p. 222

Deval is telling a friend why he was late to the skatepark. Put the pictures in the right order.
Deval erzählt einem Freund, warum er zu spät zum Skatepark gekommen ist. Bringe die Bilder in die richtige Reihenfolge.

After breakfast I made my bed and then tidied my room, as always. I was ready to go after that, but then my mum asked me to vacuum the living room floor and to walk the dog. “It won’t take long,” she said. So I vacuumed the living room and then I got ready to take our dog Snuffy outside. Then my dad said, “Please take out the rubbish on your way”. So I did that. Later, when Snuffy and I came back, my dad was outside by the car. He said, “Deval, please also ...” and I said, “...wash the car?”. And he said, “It won’t take long.” After I did that, I thought I was finished. But my mum called from the window. She asked me to empty the dishwasher. So I went inside and did that. Then I asked, “Can I go to the skatepark now?” And she said, “Yes ... after you set the table for lunch. It won’t take long.”

4 Words Jobs in the family ______ / 9

► SB, pp. 144–146, p. 267

a) **Felicia loves talking about the people in her family and their interesting jobs. Match each person with the right job (A-I). Two jobs don’t match.** *Felicia liebt es, über die Leute in ihrer Familie und ihre interessanten Jobs zu reden. Verbinde jede Person mit dem richtigen Job (A-I). Zwei Jobs passen nicht. (7 Punkte)*

1 Mum often tells us about the different animals she’s helped. ______

2 Dad works at strange times of day and night, helping fight fires. ______

3 Dad’s sister, Aunt Bess, is always working on a new software. ______

4 Uncle Will enjoys helping customers in the clothes shop. ______

5 Grandma Lily still likes cutting hair after all these years. ______

6 Grandpa John was the boss of a bank before he stopped working. ______

7 Cousin Jesse wrote a short story about Grandpa. ______

A banker
B builder
C firefighter
D hairdresser
E nurse
F programmer
G shop assistant
H vet
I writer

b) **Write your own descriptions.** *Schreibe deine eigenen Beschreibungen. (2 Punkte)*

1 Cousin Kate ____ (architect)

2 Aunt Frida ____ (baker)

► Check

5 WORDS My favourite aunt ____ / 9

► SB, pp. 266–274

Felicia is still talking about her family. Complete her statements with the words from the box. There are two words that you don't need. *Felicia redet immer noch über ihre Familie. Vervollständige ihre Aussagen mit den Wörtern aus dem Kasten. Es gibt zwei Wörter, die du nicht brauchst.*

came true • comfortable • curious • doesn't mind • earns • generous • independent • look forward to • prediction • solve • successful

I always (1) ____________________ visiting Uncle Will and Aunt Bess. I'm very (2) ____________________ about coding and programming and Aunt Bess (3) ____________________ if I ask her questions about her work. She says you have to learn to (4) ____________________ different software problems. She worked hard to learn coding. Then her dream of making video games (5) ____________________ when she got her first programming job. Now she (6) ____________________ a lot of money, she lives in a (7) ____________________ home and her game Future World is one of the most (8) ____________________ video games of the year. She's really busy, but she's so (9) ____________________ that she always makes time for me when I come to visit.

Erklär-film

6 LANGUAGE Seeing into the future ____ / 14

► SB, pp. 147–149, p. 209

Isla is sitting in a cafe one day when a strange woman sits down at her table and tells her that she can see into Isla's future. Complete her predictions with *will* or *'ll* and *won't*. *Isla sitzt eines Tages in einem Café, als sich eine fremde Frau zu ihr setzt und ihr sagt, sie könne in Islas Zukunft sehen. Vervollständige ihre Vorhersagen mit* will *oder* 'll *und* won't.

When you are 25 you (1) ____________________ (work) as a secretary in an office. Also, you (2) ____________________ (share) a flat with a friend who takes very long showers. This (3) ____________________ (not go) well. One day a grey cat named Mr Nibbles (4) ____________________ (walk) into your flat and become your best friend. At work your boss (5) ____________________ (be) horrible, and you (6) ____________________ (not earn) much money. You (7) ____________________ (not know) what to do with your life. You and Mr Nibbles (8) ____________________ (spend) many weeknights on the sofa watching boring game shows. Then you (9) ____________________ (remember) when you were little and you wanted to become a veterinarian. You (10) ____________________ (not have) enough money to study to be a vet, but your parents (11) ____________________ (help) you. After a lot of hard work your dream (12) ____________________ (come) true. Soon you (13) ____________________ (get) an exciting job in a vet clinic. You and Mr Nibbles (14) ____________________ (move) to a beautiful new house with a cat door.

► Check

Erklär-film

7 LANGUAGE I love chores ____ / 12

► SB, p. 148, p. 171, p. 210

Leo is at home with his sister and mum. Complete their dialogue with the correct form of the verb for conditional sentences (type 1). *Leo ist zuhause mit seiner Schwester und seiner Mutter. Vervollständige ihren Dialog mit der korrekten Form des Verbs für conditional sentences (type 1).*

!

Bedingungssätze (*conditional sentences*) haben zwei Teile: im Nebensatz (*if*-Teil) verwenden wir *if* + *simple present* und im Hauptsatz verwenden wir *will, 'll* oder *won't*. Der *if*-Teil kann auch hinten stehen: *If it rains tomorrow, we won't play football. We won't play football tomorrow if it rains.*

Leo Psst. Sarah! If mum (1) ____________ (forget) it's Saturday, maybe we (2) ____________ (not have) to do any chores.

Sarah If I (3) ____________ (know) mum, she (4) ____________ (not forget).

Mum Ah, here you are. Leo, it's your turn to clean the kitchen. Sarah, you can vacuum the living room.

Leo Aw, Mum! I (5) ____________ (miss) volleyball with my friends if I (6) ____________ (start) cleaning the kitchen now. Can I do something ... easier?

Mum Your friends have to do chores at home too. If you (7) ____________ (explain) it to them, I'm sure they (8) ____________ (understand).

Leo Sarah, if you (9) ____________ (swap) chores with me, I (10) ____________ (do) anything for you! ... Sarah? Where did she go?

Mum I (11) ____________ (be) in the garden if you (12) ____________ (need) me.

8 LANGUAGE At the market ____ / 5

► SB, p. 155, p. 210

Put the sentence parts in the correct order. *Bringe die Satzteile in die richtige Reihenfolge.*

1 the street market / went to / on Saturday / Luca and I /.

____

2 buys / often / second-hand clothes / Luca /.

____

3 get / delicious street food / I / some / usually /.

____

4 nearly five pounds / I / at a fish and chip stand / this time / spent /.

____

5 two T-shirts / after lunch / bought / at the big clothes stand / Luca /.

____

► Check

9 MEDIATION In a shop ____ / 11

► SB, pp. 155–156, p. 191

You're on holiday and you're looking around in a clothes shop when you hear an older German woman talking. She's having trouble communicating with the shop assistant. You offer to help. Complete the dialogue. *Du bist im Urlaub und du schaust dich in einem Klamottenladen um. Du hörst eine ältere deutsche Frau, die Schwierigkeiten hat, mit der Verkäuferin zu kommunizieren. Du bietest deine Hilfe an. Vervollständige den Dialog.*

Woman Das ist sehr lieb von dir. Ich suche eine Regenjacke. Könntest du bitte die Verkäuferin fragen, ob sie irgendwelche hat?

You Excuse me, please. (1) ____________________ ?

Assistant Yes, of course. We have them in different colours: green, blue, black and red.

You Sie sagt, (2) ____________________

Woman Ich würde gerne eine grüne Jacke haben.

You (3) ____________________

Assistant Green is a popular colour. We only have a few in size S.

You (4) ____________________

Woman Schade. Das ist mir zu klein. Gibt es eine blaue in Größe M?

You (5) ____________________

Assistant Let me see. Here's a blue one in size M.

You (6) ____________________

Woman Schön! Die blaue Jacke gefällt mir auch besser als die grüne. Was kostet sie?

You (7) ____________________

Assistant This one costs £43.95.

You (8) ____________________

Woman Das ist ein wenig teuer, aber ich brauche eine gute Regenjacke. Ich nehme sie.

You (9) ____________________

Assistant Great. Would she like to pay by card or cash?

You (10) ____________________

Woman Ich möchte mit Karte bezahlen.

You (11) ____________________

► Check

10 WRITING **A big change** ______ / 15

▶ More help, p. 85 ▶ SB, pp. 158–159

Manu is moving with his family from Brighton to Leeds in the summer. His mum has a new job there. He is writing an email to some friends to share the news together with his hopes and predictions for the future. Help him write his email. Manu's notes and the words and phrases in the box will help you.

Manu zieht im Sommer mit seiner Familie von Brighton nach Leeds. Seine Mutter hat dort einen neuen Job. Er schreibt eine E-Mail an einige Freunde, um ihnen die Nachricht sowie seine Hoffnungen und Vorhersagen mitzuteilen. Helfe ihm, seine E-Mail zu schreiben. Manus Notizen und die Wörter und Phrasen im Kasten werden dir helfen.

– Mum > better job	– my new school > be good
– Me > a new adventure	– kids and teachers > be nice
– miss Brighton	– not live near the sea
– be hard to leave you all	– have a house with a garden

I'll/It'll/They'll/We'll ... • I/it/we/they won't ... • I think/hope ... • I'm sure ... • It's a shame that ... • Let's ... • move • stay in contact • look forward to ... • sad • strange • different • interesting

!

Mit dem *will-future* sagst du, was in der Zukunft wahrscheinlich geschehen wird. Die Sätze beginnen oft mit *I think, mabye, I'm sure*.
Bilde das *will-future* mit *will* und dem Infinitiv.
I think we'll be good friends.

Hi guys,

I have some sad news. ______________________________

____

____

____

____

____

____

____

____

____

____

____

____

▶ Check

11 Study Skills Check your writing ____ / 10

► SB, p. 162, p. 196

Manu is in his new home in Leeds. Read his email to his friend Rosie in Brighton.
Manu ist in seinem neuen Zuhause in Leeds. Lies seine E-Mail an seine Freundin Rosie in Brighton.

a) **Tick (✓) yes or no.** *Hake ab (✓) ja oder nein. (2 Punkte)*

1 Does the email start and end correctly? yes ☐ no ☐

2 Is the email friendly and personal? yes ☐ no ☐

b) **Improve the underlined parts.** *Verbessere die unterstrichenen Teile. (8 Punkte)*

<u>Rosie</u>
How are you? I hope that <u>you enjoying</u> the summer break. It feels strange to be here in Leeds. Our new house is great and I've already met a few nice <u>neahbours</u>, but I miss <u>brighton</u>. Here I don't know anybody, so it's boring. And I don't feel comfortable riding my bike here because <u>I the city don't know.</u>
I'm looking <u>forword</u> to starting school. Then I'll make some friends and I won't feel so alone. I've already <u>saw</u> my new school. It's not very big, so I hope it'll be easy to meet people.
I miss you, Rosie! Let's have a video chat soon.
<u>Manu</u>

____

____

____

____

____

____

____

Bereich	Aufgabe	erreichte Punktzahl		🤩	😎	🤔	😭
listening	1	____ / 15		15–14	13–11	10–8	7–0
reading	2	____ / 5		5	4	3	2–0
words	3	____ / 8	____ /26	26–24	23–19	18–14	13–0
	4	____ / 9					
	5	____ / 9					
language	6	____ / 14	____ /31	31–28	27–22	21–16	15–0
	7	____ / 12					
	8	____ / 5					
mediation	9	____ / 11		11–10	9–8	7–6	5–0
writing	10	____ / 15		15–14	13–11	10–8	7–0
skills	11	____ / 10		10–9	8–7	6–5	4–0
Gesamt		____ / 113		113–102	101–80	79–57	56–0

► Check

Unit 6
The treasure hunt

1 LISTENING A good boy ______ / 11

▸ SB, pp. 176–181, p. 189

12

a) **Listen to a story about Laura, Miles and their dog Freddie. Number the pictures in the right order.** *Höre die Geschichte über Laura, Miles und ihren Hund Freddie. Nummeriere die Bilder in der richtigen Reihenfolge. (6 Punkte)*

b) **Listen again. Read the sentences and underline the mistakes. Write the correct words.** *Höre noch einmal zu. Lies die Sätze und unterstreiche die Fehler. Schreibe die korrekten Wörter. (5 Punkte)*

	Correction
1 Miles <u>has already taken</u> Freddie for a walk today.	hasn't taken
2 Mr O'Neill saw Freddie this morning with a younger kid.	
3 Mrs Wong told Laura's mum that she's looking for Mr O'Neill.	
4 When Freddie comes back, he barks and he's hungry.	
5 Laura and Miles decide to catch Freddie on their bikes.	
6 Freddie takes them to a field where they find Tommy.	

▸ Check

2 Reading A girl named Laura ____ / 5

► SB, p. 182, p. 190

Read the text. Then answer the questions. *Lies den Text. Dann beantworte die Fragen.*

"I'll see you at school, Jake!" Amir called as he rode away on his bike. Jake waved.
Seconds later a voice said, "Are you Jake?"
He turned and saw a girl with long brown hair and a nice smile. "Yes, that's me," he said.
"I'm Laura. I'm a ... friend of a friend," she said. "From your maths class," she added.
Jake had to think. *A friend in maths class?*
"Do you mean Emily?" he guessed.
"Yes! Emily!" she said.
They chatted about school. He was surprised how easy it was to talk to her.
"I'm so terrible at maths," she said.
Jake told her that maths was his best subject.
"Could you maybe ... help me?" she said shyly.
"Sure!" he heard himself say.
They agreed to meet at the library the next day.
Jake was very curious about this girl Laura.

"That's it! Thirty-four is the right answer."
Jake tried not to speak too loudly in the library.
"Yay! I did it! This is great," Laura said.
Jake was happy that he could help her.
"I'll be back," he said, standing up.
A few minutes later, on his way back from the toilets, he saw someone he knew.
"Hey, Emily," he said. "That's so funny. I'm just helping your friend Laura with her maths."
She looked puzzled. "I don't know anybody named Laura. Maybe you mean someone else."
"What? No," Jake said. "She's right over there." He turned and pointed at the table across the library. It was empty. Both Laura and his rucksack were gone.
"Heh?" he said. Jake thought for a moment, then he suddenly understood.
"I think she's stolen my things," he said.
"Oh no," Emily said. "Let's try to find her!"
They ran out of the library and looked around the busy square.
"There she is!" he said.
She didn't notice him as he ran to her.
"Stop right there!" Jake shouted.
She looked happy to see him. "Jake! That was really lucky! Here – I got your rucksack back."
"You what?" Jake said.
"They caught the guy. Look!" she said, pointing across the square. Jake saw two police officers putting a man into a police car.
I guess I was wrong, he thought. But he still needed some answers.
"This is Emily, from my maths class," Jake said.
"Oh ... hi," Laura said, embarrassed.
Emily looked annoyed and didn't answer.
"Who are you really?" Jake asked.
"I'm Laura. I really am. I just wanted to meet you. But it was stupid how I did it. I'm so sorry."
Jake tried to be angry, but he couldn't.
He smiled. "Well, it worked." She smiled back.

1 What did Laura tell Jake that wasn't true?

____

2 Where did they meet the next day and why?

____

3 Who else did Jake see and what did he learn from this person?

____

4 What was Jake wrong about?

____

5 Why was Laura embarrassed to see Emily?

____

► Check

3 Words Matching ____ / 7

▸ SB, pp. 274–276, p. 184

Match the words (1–8) with the right definitions and pictures (A–J). Write the letters on the correct lines. There are two definitions or pictures that don't match. *Verbinde die Wörter (1–8) mit den richtigen Definitionen und Bildern (A–J). Schreibe die korrekten Buchstaben auf die Linien. Es gibt zwei Definitionen oder Bilder die nicht passen.*

1 bush _H_
2 chant ____
3 cheat ____
4 clap ____
5 duck ____
6 pond ____
7 teammate ____
8 without ____

A

B

C the opposite of *with*

D say or shout something again and again in a sing-song way

E

F a person on your team

G speak loudly and angrily

H

I

J act in a way that's not honest or fair

4 Words Nature walk ____ / 11

▸ SB, pp. 274–276, p. 185

Complete the text with the correct words from the box. There are two more words than you need. *Vervollständige den Text mit den korrekten Wörtern aus dem Kasten. Zwei der Wörter brauchst du nicht.*

along • bench • congratulations • dandelions • good luck • grass • hike • looked up • nature reserve • pointed at • pretty • respected • shouted

Jenny and I wanted a challenge, so we decided to (1) ________ the most difficult trail in the (2) ________. Our friends thought it was a crazy idea. "(3) ________, guys!" they (4) ________ as we started walking. First we walked across a big field of tall (5) ________. There were yellow (6) ________ everywhere. "They're so (7) ________," Jenny said as she took photos. Then I (8) ________ at the mountain. "Look!", I said and (9) ________ the long trail going up. Jenny said, "Maybe this is a bit crazy." "Don't worry, we'll be fine," I said. Hours later, we sat on a (10) ________ at the end of the trail and had a snack. "That was really hard ... but fun!" Jenny said. Our friends were surprised when we got back. "(11) ________!" they said. "You did it!"

▸ Check

5 WRITING A fun class trip ______ / 15

▶ SB, pp. 176–181, p. 196

Read the email from your online penfriend in England. Write back and answer his questions. Write 80 words or more. *Lies die E-Mail von deinem online Brieffreund in England. Schreibe ihm zurück und beantworte seine Fragen. Schreibe 80 Wörter oder mehr.*

to penfriend123@example.net
from Dylan@example.net

Dear friend,
I want to tell you about a fun class trip that I went on. We visited a really cool castle. Then we did a treasure hunt in the castle gardens. The treasure hunt was the best part. The clues were really hard and some were very funny, but my team answered all of them and we found the treasure. Yay!
What was your favourite class trip? What was cool about it? Or tell me about a cool day trip with friends or family. Also, have you ever done a treasure hunt? What do you remember about it?
Bye for now, Dylan

Dear Dylan,
Thanks for your email. My favourite trip was to a ______________________

____

____

____

____

____

____

____

Bereich	Aufgabe	erreichte Punktzahl	🤩	😎	🤔	😭
listening	1	______ / 11	11–10	9–8	7–6	5–0
reading	2	______ / 5	5	4	3	2–0
words	3	______ / 7 } ______ / 18	18–16	15–12	11–9	8–0
	4	______ / 11				
writing	5	______ / 15	15–14	13–11	10–8	7–0
Gesamt		______ / 49	49–44	43–34	33–25	24–0

▶ Check

More help

▶ Unit 1, page 12

8 Writing Gita and Arun in Edinburgh ____ / 15

▶ SB, pp. 30–31

Look at the pictures. Then write the story about this sister and brother on their family holiday. Write 100 words or more. Use the simple past. The words in the box can help you. *Schaue die Bilder an. Schreibe dann die Geschichte über den Familienurlaub dieser Geschwister. Schreibe 100 Wörter oder mehr. Benutze das simple past. Die Wörter im Kasten können dir helfen.*

to arrive • to dance • to get off • to see • to shop • to stay • to watch • busy • cheap • cool • excited • exciting • free • fun • clothes • costume • mask • (street) musician • street festival • vampire

Their train arrived at the station in Edinburgh, and Gita and Arun ____________________

____

At McPurdy's Hostel, ____________________

____

Later the family walked around in the city and ____________________

____

They went to a second-hand clothes shop and ____________________

____

That evening, Gita and Arun ____________________

____

____

▶ Check

► Unit 2, page 19

7 WRITING One of my friends ____ / 15

► SB, pp. 46–52, p. 214

Look at the online post about someone's friend. Write a post about one of your friends. *Schaue den Post über eine Freundin von jemandem an. Schreibe einen Beitrag über eine Freundin oder einen Freund von dir.*

Write about:
- what he/she is like (looks, personality)
- how you met
- two reasons why you are happy to be friends with this person

You can use the words in the box or your own.
Write 80 words or more.

Schreibe über:
- *was für ein Typ er/sie ist (Aussehen, Persönlichkeit)*
- *wie ihr euch kennengelernt habt*
- *zwei Gründe, warum du froh bist, mit dieser Person befreundet zu sein*

evie_sundowner43

evie_sundowner43 Ginny and I met at music school last year. She's so creative and she always listens to my ideas. We often write songs …

Du kannst die Wörter im Kasten verwenden oder deine eigene. Schreibe 80 Wörter oder mehr.

black • blond • blue • braces • brown • dark • curly • eyes • glasses • hair • long • red • short • straight	
brave • clever • confident • creative • fair • friendly • funny • generous • independent • hard-working • kind • patient • practical • relaxed • reliable • shy • sociable	
The first time we met was …• I think we met at/when … • We became friends when/after …	
He/She	helps me • listens to me • never gets too angry/excited/stressed • teaches me a lot
We	have fun together • laugh a lot • like the same things • share everything

► Check

► Unit 3, page 27

9 WRITING It's going to be cool! ____ / 15

► SB, pp. 80–83

You're texting with a classmate who wasn't at the school assembly today. Look at the timetable and answer her questions about sports week. Name at least three activities that you're going to do. For each activity think about what, when and where. *Du schreibst eine SMS an eine Schulkameradin, die heute nicht bei der Schulversammlung war. Schaue den Zeitplan an und beantworte ihre Fragen zur Sports Week. Nenne mindestens drei Aktivitäten, die du tun wirst. Für jede Aktivität denke an was, wann und wo.*

SPORTS WEEK			
	in the ASSEMBLY HALL	**in the GYM**	**at the SPORTS FIELD**
on MON	at 12:45 Sports Week assembly	1:00 Fun with gymnastics 2:30 Gymnastics level 1	1:00 Football level 1 2:30 Golf level 1
on TUES	at 12:45 Table tennis level 1 at 2:15 Table tennis level 2	12:45 Basketball level 1 2:15 Volleyball level 1	12:45 Cricket level 1 2:15 Tennis level 1
on WED	at 12:45 Judo level 1 at 2:15 Judo level 2	12:45 Volleyball level 2 2:15 Gymnastics level 2	12:45 Football level 2 2:15 Tennis level 2
on THURS	at 12:45 Boxing level 1 at 2:15 Boxing level 2	12:45 Basketball level 2 2:15 Gymnastics final	12:45 Cricket level 2 2:15 Cricket final
on FRI	at 12:45 Table tennis final at 2:15 Judo final	12:45 Basketball final 2:15 Volleyball final	12:45 Football final 2:15 Tennis final

Did they talk about sports week at the assembly today? What activities are you going to do? Hey, let's do an activity together! Maybe tennis, if it's in the timetable?

Yes, ______________________________

____

On Monday I'm going to ______________________________

____

On Tuesday ______________________________

____

Would you like to ______________________________

______________________________?

And I like your your idea too! We could ______________________________

____

► Check

▶ Unit 4, page 61

10 WRITING A birthday celebration ____ / 15

▶ SB, pp. 114–117, pp. 122–123

Ben and his dad have travelled to Bristol to celebrate his grandma's 70th birthday. Ben's friend Allie texts him late that evening. Read Ben's diary notes and answer Allie's questions. You can use the ideas in the box or your own. *Ben ist mit seinem Vater nach Bristol gereist, um den 70. Geburtstag seiner Großmutter zu feiern. Bens Freundin Allie schreibt ihm spät am Abend eine SMS. Lies Bens Tagebuchnotizen und beantworte Allies Fragen. Du kannst die Ideen im Kasten oder deine eigenen verwenden.*

Granny Ann's birthday

today	tomorrow
11 a.m. – arrive at Auntie Nicky's house	10 a.m. – go hiking with Granny Ann
2 p.m. – surprise Granny with birthday cake	12 a.m. – Dad makes fish and chips for lunch
5:30 p.m. – have big family dinner	1:30 p.m. – visit art museum with cousins
7:30 p.m. – play board games	4 p.m. – Dad and I drive back to Brighton

birthday cake • beef/lamb/pork • to arrive early/on time • to blow out the candles • to give sb. a present • to have sth. for dinner • to make a wish • to surprise sb. • to thank sb.

Hey Ben, how's it going in Bristol? When did you guys arrive? Did your grandma have a nice birthday? Tell me about it! ✓

Hey Allie, it's going great. We arrived ______________________

____

We had a fun day. In the afternoon we surprised ______________________

____

____

At 5:30 we ______________________

____

Later we ______________________

______________________ ✓

Sounds cool! What's your plan for tomorrow? What time are you going to drive back? ✓

Tomorrow morning I'm going to ______________________

____

Then Dad is ______________________

____

After that my cousins and I are ______________________

____

At 4 p.m. ______________________

______________________ ✓

▶ Check

▶ Unit 5, page 75

10 WRITING **A big change** ____ / 15

▶ SB, pp. 158–159

Manu is moving with his family from Brighton to Leeds in the summer. His mum has a new job there. He is writing an email to some friends to share the news together with his hopes and predictions for the future. Help him write his email. Manu's notes and the words and phrases in the box will help you. *Manu zieht im Sommer mit seiner Familie von Brighton nach Leeds. Seine Mutter hat dort einen neuen Job. Er schreibt eine E-Mail an einige Freunde, um ihnen die Nachricht sowie seine Hoffnungen und Vorhersagen mitzuteilen. Helfe ihm, seine E-Mail zu schreiben. Manus Notizen und die Wörter und Phrasen im Kasten werden dir helfen.*

– Mum > better job	– my new school > be good
– Me > a new adventure	– kids and teachers > be nice
– miss Brighton	– not live near the sea
– be hard to leave you all	– have a house with a garden

I'll/It'll/They'll/We'll … • I/it/we/they won't … •
I think/hope … • I'm sure … •
It's a shame that … • Let's … •
move • stay in contact • look forward to … •
sad • strange • different • interesting

!

Mit dem *will-future* sagst du, was in der Zukunft wahrscheinlich geschehen wird. Die Sätze beginnen oft mit *I think, mabye, I'm sure*.
Bilde das *will-future* mit *will* und dem Infinitiv.
I think we'll be good friends.

Hi guys,

I have some sad news. My mum has a new job in Leeds, so we're going to move there in the summer.

Mum will ____

____

____

I hope that my new school will be ____

____

____

It's a shame that we won't ____

____

____

____

Let's stay in contact, guys! I look forward to ____

____

____

Manu

▶ Check

▶ Unit 6, page 80

5 Writing A fun class trip ____ / 15

▶ SB, pp. 176–181, p. 196

Read the email from your online penfriend in England. Write back and answer his questions. Write 80 words or more. The words and phrases in the box will help you.

Lies die E-Mail von deinem online Brieffreund in England. Schreibe ihm zurück und beantworte seine Fragen. Schreibe 80 Wörter oder mehr. Die Wörter und Phrasen im Kasten werden dir helfen.

to penfriend123@example.net

from Dylan@email.com

Dear friend,

I want to tell you about a fun class trip that I went on. We visited a really cool castle. Then we did a treasure hunt in the castle gardens. The treasure hunt was the best part. The clues were really hard and some were very funny, but my team answered all of them and we found the treasure. Yay!

What was your favourite class trip? What was cool about it? Or tell me about a cool day trip with friends or family. Also, have you ever done a treasure hunt? What do you remember about it?

Bye for now,

Dylan

I once did a cool day trip to/with ... • I went there with ... • My favourite class trip was to ... • It was really fun/cool/interesting/ ... because ... • First we ..., then we ... • We were there for ...
The best part was (when we) ... • What I liked most was (when we) ... • I'll never forget when ...
I've been on a treasure hunt once/two times/a few times/ ... • I remember that there was/were ... • The clues were ... • At the end the treasure was ... • I've never been on a treasure hunt, but I've ... • I'd like to ...

Dear Dylan,

Thanks for your email. My favourite trip was to a ____________________

Cover

Cornelsen/Personen am Strand: Anja Poehlmann, Strandhäuschen: Shutterstock.com/JoolsW

Illustrationen

Cornelsen/Evelt Yanait, Advocate Art: S. 7/2a, S. 7/2b, S. 7/3a, S. 7/5b, S. 7/6a, S. 7/6b, S. 8/o.r., S. 9/5, S. 9/6, S. 9/9, S. 12, S. 14, S. 15, S. 16, S. 20/m.r., S. 22, S. 24, S. 25, S. 26, S. 31/2b, S. 31/3a, S. 31/5a, S. 31/5b, S. 31/6a, S. 31/6b, S. 35, S. 48, S. 53, S. 56, S. 64/m., S. 68, S. 71/o., S. 72, S. 73, S. 74, S. 77, S. 81; **Cornelsen/Irina Zinner:** S. 3/6, S. 29, S. 64/u.r..

Abbildungen

S. 1: Cornelsen/Inhouse/Anne Weingarten; **S. 2:** PEFC Deutschland e.V.; **S. 3**/1: Cornelsen/Anja Poehlmann; S. 3/2: Cornelsen/Anja Poehlmann; S. 3/3: Cornelsen/Anja Poehlmann; S. 3/4: Cornelsen/Anja Poehlmann; S. 3/5: Cornelsen/Anja Poehlmann; **S. 7**/1a: stock.adobe.com/RP; S. 7/1b: stock.adobe.com/RP; S. 7/4a: stock.adobe.com/RP; S. 7/4b: stock.adobe.com/Tarik GOK; **S. 8**/Emoji: Shutterstock.com/Yefym Turkin; **S. 11:** stock.adobe.com/David Matthew Lyons; **S. 13:** Shutterstock.com/Yefym Turkin; **S. 17:** Shutterstock.com/PeopleImages.com - Yuri A; S. 18: Shutterstock.com/Phovoir; **S. 19**/Icons: stock.adobe.com/mukhamad; S. 19/o.r.: Shutterstock.com/SeventyFour; **S. 20**/Emojis: Shutterstock.com/Yefym Turkin; **S. 21**/A: stock.adobe.com/matteo; S. 21/B: mauritius images/Mara Brandl/imageBROKER; S. 21/C: stock.adobe.com/Mark; S. 21/D: stock.adobe.com/chika_milan; S. 21/E: stock.adobe.com/Africa Studio; S. 21/F: stock.adobe.com/laura; S. 21/G: stock.adobe.com/HildaWeges; S. 21/H: stock.adobe.com/Diana Vyshniakova; **S. 23:** stock.adobe.com/akkash; **S. 28:** Shutterstock.com/Yefym Turkin; **S. 31**/1a: stock.adobe.com/RP; S. 31/1b: stock.adobe.com/RP; S. 31/4a: stock.adobe.com/RP; S. 31/4b: stock.adobe.com/Tarik GOK; **S. 38**/A: stock.adobe.com/matteo; S. 38/B: mauritius images/Mara Brandl/imageBROKER; S. 38/C: stock.adobe.com/Mark; S. 38/D: stock.adobe.com/chika_milan; S. 38/E: stock.adobe.com/Africa Studio; S. 38/F: stock.adobe.com/laura; S. 38/G: stock.adobe.com/HildaWeges; S. 38/H: stock.adobe.com/Diana Vyshniakova; **S. 42**/1: stock.adobe.com/Frank; S. 42/2: stock.adobe.com/IndiaPix; S. 42/3: stock.adobe.com/Paul Maguire; S. 42/4: Shutterstock.com/Fevziie; **S. 44:** stock.adobe.com/Mirador; **S. 55**/1: stock.adobe.com/Frank; S. 55/2: stock.adobe.com/IndiaPix; S. 55/3: stock.adobe.com/Paul Maguire; S. 55/4: Shutterstock.com/Fevziie; **S. 57**/1: stock.adobe.com/volff; S. 57/2: Shutterstock.com/Sayouna; S. 57/3: stock.adobe.com/steftach; S. 57/4: Shutterstock.com/Fotofermer; S. 57/5: Shutterstock.com/mexrix; S. 57/6: Shutterstock.com/Adisa; S. 57/7: stock.adobe.com/Vector Nazmul; S. 57/8: Shutterstock.com/N Ahmad; S. 57/o.r.: stock.adobe.com/POSMGUYS; **S. 58:** stock.adobe.com/zinkevych; **S. 60**/m.: Shutterstock.com/Vector Tradition; S. 60/o.r.: stock.adobe.com/PeoplesDesignStudios; **S. 62**/Emoijis: Shutterstock.com/Yefym Turkin; S. 62/m.r.: stock.adobe.com/Mirador; S. 62/o.l.: stock.adobe.com/Kiattisak; **S. 63**/m.l.: stock.adobe.com/Ncorp; S. 63/m.r.: stock.adobe.com/linortis; S. 63/o.m.: stock.adobe.com/simona; S. 63/u.l.: stock.adobe.com/ghazii; S. 63/u.m.: stock.adobe.com/Nicholas Felix/peopleimages.com; S. 63/u.r.: stock.adobe.com/Seventyfour; **S. 64**/o.r.: stock.adobe.com/SynthexUA; **S. 65:** mauritius images/Prostock-studio/Alamy Stock Photos; **S. 66:** stock.adobe.com/T Hover/peopleimages.com; **S. 67:** mauritius images/Caia Image; **S. 69**/A: stock.adobe.com/pilipphoto; S. 69/B: stock.adobe.com/Dragana Gordic; S. 69/C: stock.adobe.com/Halfpoint; S. 69/D: stock.adobe.com/Monkey Business; S. 69/E: stock.adobe.com/anandart; S. 69/F: stock.adobe.com/Ian; S. 69/G: stock.adobe.com/colnihko; **S. 70**/Dylan: stock.adobe.com/alfa27; S. 70/Eve: stock.adobe.com/mimagephotos; S. 70/Jenny: stock.adobe.com/Woraphon; S. 70/Manu: stock.adobe.com/IndiaPix; **S. 71**/m.r.: stock.adobe.com/Andrii Nekrasov; **S. 76:** Shutterstock.com/Yefym Turkin; **S. 79**/A: stock.adobe.com/NikLemesh; S. 79/B: Shutterstock.com/Elena Krivorotova; S. 79/E: stock.adobe.com/EnginKorkmaz; S. 79/H: Shutterstock.com/YARphotographer; S. 79/I: mauritius images/Rawpixel Ltd/Alamy/Alamy Stock Photos; **S. 80:** Shutterstock.com/Yefym Turkin; **S. 82**/Icons: stock.adobe.com/mukhamad; S. 82/o.r.: Shutterstock.com/SeventyFour.

Trackliste

	Track	Titel	Seite	Aufgabe
Unit 1	01	**Sharing holiday stories**	7	1
Unit 2	02	**Interesting people**	14	1
Unit 3	03	**Planning a visit**	21	1
Unit 4	04	**Celebrating with friends**	55	1
Speaking	05	**A celebration**	63	1
	06	**Giving directions**	64	2
	07	**An interesting person**	65	3
	08	**A good teacher**	66	4
	09	**Making plans**	67	5
	10	**In a clothes shop**	68	6
Unit 5	11	**I want to be a …**	69	1
Unit 6	12	**A good boy**	77	1